# AN ABSENCE OF RUINS

## ALSO BY H. ORLANDO PATTERSON

Fiction:
*The Children of Sisyphus*
*Die the Long Day*

Non-Fiction:
*The Sociology of Slavery*
*Ethnic Chauvinism: The Reactionary Impulse*
*Slavery and Social Death*
*Freedom in the Making of Western Culture*
*The Ordeal of Integration*
*Rituals of Blood: Consequences of Slavery in Two American Centuries*

AN ABSENCE OF RUINS

ORLANDO PATTERSON

INTRODUCTION BY JEREMY POYNTING

PEEPAL TREE

First published in Great Britain in 1967
by Hutchinson & Co
This new edition published in 2012
Peepal Tree Press Ltd
17 King's Avenue
Leeds LS6 1QS
England

Introduction: Jeremy Poynting

ISBN13: 9781845231040

Supported by
ARTS COUNCIL
ENGLAND

# JEREMY POYNTING

## INTRODUCTION

When it was first published in 1967, *An Absence of Ruins* was noticed in the Caribbean mainly because it satirised some identifiable members of the Jamaican intellectual community.[1] It was seen as belonging to a group of novels (works by V.S. Naipaul and Garth St. Omer were the other offenders) categorised as negative or nihilistic.[2] Bridget Jones, in the most extensive examination so far of Patterson's fiction,[3] wrote of his "scrupulous nihilism". In tracing influences from Camus and Sartre she described Patterson's work as interesting, but suspected that "Patterson was too calculatingly intelligent to be a good novelist".[4] The criticism was double-edged. By the time of Jones's critique, John Hearne's sloganistic dismissal of Patterson's fiction as "The Novel as Sociology as Bore" (in reference to Patterson's third novel, *Die the Long Day*[5]) seems to have been readily adopted by those who wanted to slap the young upstart down. The titling of Jones's essay ("Some French Influences..."), also seemed to say that, really, Patterson was not being West Indian enough.

*An Absence of Ruins* undoubtedly ran counter to a number of growing orthodoxies. It ridiculed the manifestos of peasant authenticity that began in Lamming's *The Pleasures of Exile*;[6] Patterson's Jamaican peasants appear briefly, trudging to their fields with "weary resignation" – with a provocative dig when the main character refuses "to believe that they could remain so silent. Were these not his folk? Were they not the happy, simple people of the countryside. Why did they not shout with earthy gusto at each other...?" (p. 127. Page references are to this edition). It is clear, too, from his recorded interventions in the Caribbean Artists Movement, that Patterson regarded the calls for an explicitly Caribbean nativist aesthetic as a symptom of the anxieties of middle-class cultural nationalism;[7] Patterson locates his novel in what would be (and was) taken to be a European aesthetic. Indeed, the novel displays its literary precursors very openly: Dostoyevsky, Camus and Sartre (though also – and not generally noted in the reviews – the work of Frantz Fanon).

There are other elements of risk. If *The Children of Sisyphus* portrays characters for whom, as Kwame Dawes writes, we want to hope,[8] *An Absence of Ruins* spends most of its space within the head of a calculatedly unsympathetic character. And if *The Children of Sisyphus* could be criticised for the intrusions of Patterson's authorial voice into the reflections of his proletarian characters, in *An Absence of Ruins* there's not much sign of an author distinct from the point of view of the main character, Alexander Blackman. This seems to have led Bridget Jones, at least, to assume that the voice of the central character was, in a fairly unmediated way, Patterson's. For instance, she sees the use of passages from Bishop King (in *The Children of Sisyphus*) and Donne (in *An Absence of Ruins*) as pointing to Patterson having "a magical view of English Literature".[9] This seems to me a reading that ignores context. In the first instance, Patterson uses the reference as a character-revealing device, in the second as part of a literary parody.

*An Absence of Ruins* is a politically engaged novel and an aesthetically daring one. Indeed, there is nothing like it in Anglophone Caribbean fiction. It is a novel that simultaneously plots an absorbing and often comic narrative, and makes a fundamental criticism of the whole direction of the West Indian novel. It is boldly modernist in what it does with the instabilities of the narrative voice, with its use of metafictions and with the ambiguity it creates between the identities of the author and the central character. In this respect it looks forward to a novel such as Percival Everett's *Erasure* (2001) – though of course James Joyce's *Ulysses* (1921) had shown the way in its stylistic journey through literary history.

The aesthetics and the politics go hand in hand. They are both motivated by Patterson's fiercely critical attitude to the characteristics of the West Indian, and more particularly the Jamaican middle class, whether as the country's ruling class, its "radical" intellectuals, or its writers. For him, the Jamaican middle class was notable for its "smugness", and the middle-class-led post-independence governments from 1962 to 1967 for their coloniality, social conservatism, pro-plantocratic stance and failure to develop the economy beyond increasing middle-class employment. However, unlike *The Children of Sisyphus*, we don't see this class in *An Absence of Ruins*. What we do see is a group of radical intellectuals who are supposedly leading the opposition to this state of affairs. Here, the novel mercilessly exposes what Patterson saw as the delusions and pretensions of this group, vocally committed to radical change, but still trapped by their shaping as a colonially educated elite and by the class location this brings them. Specifically, the novel satirises the campus-based New World Group in ways that connect to Walter Rodney's criticism of the group as armchair socialists who lacked contact with the working class.[10] We first see the group behaving as if they were a vanguardist Leninist party trying to discipline Alex for his political backsliding – his withdrawal from political activism, as defined by the group. In the next chapter, members of the group appear as socialites partying and engaged in casual sexual adventures.

But above all, *An Absence of Ruins* is an assault on the "bourgeois" Caribbean novel. For Patterson, the role of the middle-class novelist in purporting to speak for the mass of the Caribbean's working and peasant classes was evidently analogous to the role of the Jamaican middle classes in "leading" the masses through the two competing bourgeois nationalist parties and through the trade union movement. (The eponymous Bustamente Industrial Trade Union led by a man who had made his money from moneylending suffices to make the point.)

Patterson was not the first Caribbean author to focus on the distance between writer and subject and express discomfort over it. In George Lamming's *Season of Adventure* (1960), there is the much noted moment when the novelist steps out from behind the narrative and speaks directly to the reader, unburdening his guilt over failing his "half-brother", Powell, the steelbandsman. Powell has been driven to desperate criminality, the writer believes, because he, the writer, has abandoned him after colonial education separated him from working class life.[11] Patterson adopts a broader and more complex fictional strategy to deal with these contradictions. In *The Children of Sisyphus* he defends himself by taking on the role of the novelist as "a kind of sociologist", a discoverer who can tell a largely middle-class readership about a world it doesn't know or understand. In *An Absence of Ruins* Patterson confronts the situation by creating a "novel" within the novel that serves several functions: satirising the class position of the West Indian writer, ironising himself as inescapably of that class, and parodying (in the widest sense of the word) the very texture, aesthetics and angle of vision of the West Indian novel. The parody is done so faithfully and exactly that contemporary reviewers missed it.

At best, earlier critiques acknowledged the novel's ambition, but by missing its metafictional strategies, saw only solemnity and unevenness. My view is that *An Absence of Ruins* is an altogether a more ludic, multivoiced (poetic, poignant, satirical, and frequently darkly comic), and formally coherent novel than has previously been recognised. The world of its 1960s' politics has passed, but the challenge it poses to the perspectives and aesthetics of the Caribbean novel is as provocative and original as it ever was. It is not a novel that reveals itself casually; it challenges how attentively we read and query our assumptions. The chapter dealing with the failed relationship between Alexander and his wife suggests familiarity with the work of the radical phenomenological psychiatrist R.D. Laing. Indeed, Laing's starting point in *The Politics of Experience* ("'My experience of you' is just another form of words for 'you-as-I-experience-you'"[12]) offers a salutary starting point, in the context of earlier misreadings, for thinking about the relationship between the reader and the text, particularly one as complex in its surface signals as this one.

What remains ambivalent, for instance, is how far Patterson ironises his own position as a novelist with ambitions (fairly soon to be abandoned) to bring something new to the West Indian novel, who is not afraid of writing an "impure" novel of ideas, in the face of condemnation by the "bourgeois" advocates of "pure" fiction such as John Hearne or Kenneth Ramchand. On the one hand, Patterson's engagement with contemporary Caribbean debates about African origins and survivals, racial essentialism, and how to relate to the region's history appears serious, and his use of Sartrean analytical categories to explore Alexander Blackman's consciousness seems offered at face value. On the other hand, the

8

Sartrean episode at the beginning of the novel is structurally part of a series of metafictional parodies, and later in the novel, when Alexander Blackman is shown engaging in Sartrean self-analysis, the result is self-confusion rather than clarity.

Whilst the character who is and is not the author is a familiar, foregrounded element in the modernist novel, it's a rarer feature in West Indian fiction (*In the Castle of My Skin* is another obvious exception), dominated as it is by the mass of quasi-autobiographical writing presented in an un-self-reflexive way. But *where* Patterson is in the novel has less to do with biography than with the dynamics of the novel's aesthetic structure, particularly in relation to the interplay between third and first person modes of narration. This is the means whereby Patterson simultaneously advances the plot towards its tragicomic conclusion, creates a parodic simulacrum of the West Indian novel and locates a fictional version of himself within the text in a self-critical and self-deprecating way.

We might remember the self-mocking portrait of the naïve student who turns up to lecture the Rastafarian brethren in *The Children of Sisyphus* as a clue to Patterson's intentions.[13] To state the obvious, Alex Blackman is not Patterson, and for much of the novel this is very clear; but in creating Blackman, he offers an intensive and inward dramatisation of how the world looks to a particular man, shaped by colonial education and by his individual family origins (a mother who fathered him), who is just beginning to question his deepest, but in reality most fragile, assumptions – a character who just happens to share some points of identity with Patterson himself. In an essay (part of which was published in *Savacou* in 1972), Patterson wrote that when the West Indian intellectual "begins to worry about the problem of national and racial identity... It is at this point that he takes up writing, the peculiar cultural reflex of the West Indian abroad..."[14] It is a mocking exaggeration from which Patterson cannot, of course, exonerate himself.

He introduces this element of self-reflection into the novel by making Blackman's story share some parameters with his own, most crucially that they are both Jamaicans returning to the island after years of study and teaching in England. The pertinence of

9

this experience to the narrative is made plain in an article pub-lished in *New Left Review* in 1965. There Patterson wrote: "It is perhaps for this reason that what impresses a Jamaican most on returning home after a few years abroad – as I did recently – is the marginality of his society. It immediately becomes clear to him that if ever a society is on the fringe it is his own." This experience led Patterson to pose the questions which he believed every Jamaican must ask himself: "What is a Jamaican? Who is he? Has he a past? Is there any meaningful way in which he can define himself, culturally or personally, within the present?"[15]

Alexander Blackman asks himself these questions, particularly regarding his own self-definition and his scope for choice. There are clearly points, too, where the perceptions of the character and of his creator do coincide, though Patterson as public intellectual, and Patterson as novelist are obviously engaged in different orders of discourse. For example, there are connections between the satirical portrayal of the leftist group in the novel, and the view Patterson expresses in his *New Left Review* article that: "It is now fashionable among Jamaican intellectuals to predict a mass rising in the near future. This has been going on for some time. My own analysis does not support such a view and I entertain very thin hopes for such a movement in the immediate future." For Patterson, Jamaica was not even neo-colonial in the way that described much of newly independent Africa or Asia, but "politi-cally far more backward".[16]

This is not too different from Alexander Blackman's view, though he expresses his alienation in wholly personal terms: his fear of being "swallowed up" by this "damn little island", "so barren, so claustrophobic" (p. 47). In the novel, Blackman's recog-nition that he's reached a dead-end sends him off on a journey towards existential nullity; he is Patterson's imagining of the absurd, sometimes comic, sometimes moving, responses of a self-obsessed character who defends his solipsism by saying, "I can only think about myself if I am not to go crazy about everything else" (p. 150). By contrast, Patterson ended his *New Left Review* essay with the thought: "The Jamaican mass-movement has yet to appear. The only consolation is that when the revolution finally does come, there will be no British rulers around to act as scapegoats". This was

Patterson in c1965. By the early 1970s, though no doubt even more certain that there was no mass revolutionary movement round the corner, and no less sceptical about the radical credentials of the middle-class leadership of the 1972 Michael Manley government, in the real world Patterson worked as an advisor to that government on projects to ameliorate poverty. Yet, in the writing of *An Absence of Ruins* – and it is one of the elements that gives the novel its continuing life – one suspects the presence of a young author who was at crisis point in the pragmatics of his political convictions, who was wondering whether there was a future for him (whether there was a point, indeed) in the writing of fiction, and who felt isolated in feeling that he could not belong to any of the groups that competed for intellectual space in Jamaica, whether left-wing nationalist, Afro-centric, cultural nationalist, or the mimic bourgeois elite. Those anxieties are present in ironised form in the character of Alexander Blackman.

The realisation of Blackman's character, the narrative's trajectory and the metafictional satire are achieved through the novel's two modes of telling – the formal alternation between first and third person – and the way the relationship between these modes changes at different points in the novel. The purpose of this alternation seems to have been missed in previous readings. Bridget Jones, for instance, sees the first person passages as simply a rambling and self-indulgent portrayal of Blackman's inner angst and the shifts in tone as deficiencies in consistency.

But the relationship between the two modes is dynamic. The third person episodes, as one might expect, provide a more "reliable" picture of how flawed and inadequate Alex Blackman is as a human being and as a writer; at the same time as they give a context and a jumping-off point for the fictions of the first person chapters.

In Chapter 2, for instance, we get a picture of a selfish, immature man who is incapable of decisive action, who admits that his marriage was based on possessive jealousy, who comes to tell his wife Pauline yet again that they are finished, but ends up in bed with her, engaging in his self-obsessed way in her further humiliation. He evades responsibility by blaming his state of mind both on his situation as a returnee to Jamaica, whose choice is "self-imposed ignorance or the confrontation with barrenness" (p. 57) and on the

11

defects of his personality as "a coward, afraid of all action, of all commitment. But I don't mind. I'm most at ease with myself this way". At this point, all we can see in his honesty is self-indulgence.

This connection to wider issues provides a link to Chapter 3 – the meeting at Edward's where Alex meets his "inquisitors", and the party at Joyce's, where the only working-class presence is the music. Here, in the context of the self-deceiving frauds of the group – Lloyd's demagoguery, Edward's radical posturing, the "phoneyness" of Fitzmaurice, Joyce's claim that she seduces husbands in order to reform Jamaican wives in their ways of raising boys – Alex begins to look rather more sympathetic. We can at least see why he should be in a state of self-questioning uncertainty.

But the move between first and third person sets up more than just a contrast between internal and external views. This is first signalled in Chapter 1 at the point where the "I" narration ends in a series of ellipses and switches to third person narration when Richard, alias Alexander, is told to go to bed by his mother: "Suddenly I felt sick. I snatched myself out of bed and…/ 'Darling, it is time for you to get some sleep' (p. 45)". What Alex/Richard has supposedly been doing is writing up his diary, but his mother's comment, "Seems more like a book you're writing", hints that he is in fact writing something rather different. Though there is a point later in the novel when first person passages can be read more plausibly as a diary (where "I" and "he" more closely coincide), in the main, Alex can be seen as shaping the supposed events of his life into a fiction, or even writing total fantasy. These metafictional passages work at a number of levels. They reveal Alex's innermost feelings in a way that his directly verbalised thoughts cannot do. In almost all of the first person narratives there is, for instance, a movement from wishful thinking to its collapse, when reality can no longer be kept at bay. But beyond the role of these first person episodes as a means of revealing character, there's something else going on, and this is not just Patterson's ironic reflection on the general propensity of West Indian intellectuals to want to write, but a specific parodying or referencing of particular writers as a means of building a critique of the existing West Indian novel.

On the evidence of his interactions with his mother, Alex, though thirty, is clearly an extremely immature and indecisive "mummy's boy" who does as he is told and puts on his pyjamas (and then takes them off again) and goes to bed. There he begins daydreaming a continuation of the "I" narrative we might at first have assumed to be "true" from the beginning of the chapter, until he is woken by a wet dream. At this point, the reader who has picked up the clues should begin to suspect that some at least of the "I" narrative exists in Alex's imagination, particularly when we realise that he, Richard, son of Miss Rebecca Jones, has reinvented himself with a name he thinks is more appropriate for the author of a doctoral dissertation on "The Contribution of the Negro to Western Civilisation", a title that itself tells us a good deal.

In this episode, before his mother's interruption, where the narrator visits the sea, a bar and a brothel, and describes his isolation in the aridity of the natural world, we have Alex portraying himself as the existential anti-hero, alien in the landscape and then as an alien amongst the people. (This section, when extracted in *New Left Review*, was entitled "The Alien".[17]) The style is taut, spare, tight-lipped, tough, suggesting the objective, self-analytical precision of a Sartrean figure, and as Bridget Jones notes, there is a very obvious homage to Sartre's *La Nausée* in the act of staring at the roots of a tree in the very first paragraph.[18] Watching the sea, Alex has his character enact a being-and-nothingness moment:

> For the sea is the only place I know in the face of which I can be absolutely certain that I will not think of it. Its essence is separateness, which at least ensures the possibility of other things. There I can dream and lust and search eternally.
> So for the rest of the afternoon […] I lost count of consciousness. I became a vacancy. (p. 38)

Later, when his character rejoins the world, a world immersed in bad faith, to go among "the multitude, who had remained earthbound, committed to their earthly existence simply by default" (p. 40), there are giveaway elements that point to Alex's middle-classness and suggest an element of fantasy in, for instance, the image of himself as the uncouth troublemaker who spits in the bar (this is the Alex who does what his mother tells him). There is a description of ska music (and Patterson has recently been on record speaking of how much he always admired Toots and the Maytals, who were always as much ska and revival as reggae[19]) as "a harsh, pulsatile ubiquitous ode to monotony…" (p. 40), and of people dancing. This demonstrates both Alex's fragmented mode of perception, and his conflicted class relations to the dancers:

> their bodies bent from the waist, their torsos bobbing up and down in an agile, repetitive bowing: necks stretching in and out like irate turkeys, hands alternating between their thighs and their chins like panting long-distance runners. Yet, despite the awkward angularity of their movements, despite the appear-ance of an excessive display of energy, an innate sense of rhythm seemed to smooth over everything making the dance something beautiful to watch. Its vulgarity mocking itself, this ska, a droll, defiant beautification of clumsiness. (p. 42)

The same kind of fragmentation of body parts is offered in Alex's description of the whore, whose "vulgarity" is part of her attraction, but where, like the beer, expectation precedes a "rush into emptiness", his moment of nausea, his panic that even the feeling of vacancy may be an illusion. There's a connection here (in the emphasis on perception, its disjointedness and restriction to surfaces) with George Lamming's *Of Age and Innocence* (1958) and the character of the middle-class intellectual Mark Kennedy, who, like Alex, has returned from England to the Caribbean and been decentered by the experience.[20]

In the next episode of "I" narration in Chapter 4, describing the brief but "beautiful days" with the un-named woman who is a version of Carmen, the woman who propositions Alex at the party in Chapter 3, the style and tone are noticeably different. Here is Alex trying on a different narrative voice and persona, one that I suspect parodies Patterson's old adversary, John Hearne, in the poetic expansiveness of the style, the man-of-the-world confi-dences, the display of finer feelings in the quotation from John Donne (which also plays with the idea of nothingness, in "things which are not" (p. 81)). There is a passage in Hearne's *Land of the Living* (1961) which, whilst it may not be Patterson's source, suggests the kind of prose and angle of view that is being parodied. This is Hearne's Stefan Mahler writing about the begin-nings of his relationship to Joan Culpepper:

The world outside ourselves was so irrelevant that we did not find that it trespassed. The necessities of work and social contact were hardly considered any more than the habits of hygiene or the humdrum domestic obligations. In those days, I remember, we both took a great deal of childish pleasure in that capacity lovers discover for making themselves invisible to others without absence. Totally absorbed in each other, we managed to keep our infatuation as secret as the courtship of two wild animals. And we did this, I think, as much from a sense of protection as from a spirit of innocent mischief... [21]

Alex, in the same spirit of self-congratulatory worldliness, the same easy and unreflective acceptance of middle-class socialite pleasures, writes how:

They were beautiful days. They were careless days. Irresponsible days. Days of idleness. Days without thought. Days devoid of anticipation, contemptuous of the future. Days without memory, oblivious of the past. Each moment was taken for what it was, accepted on its own terms, rejected on its own terms.

We tasted everything that was in the offing – passion, laughter, poetry, picnics by the sea, walks in the mountains – we chewed upon them. What we cared for we swallowed. What we didn't like we spat out. But, really, it mattered little whether we swallowed or rejected, for they were all the same, simply a moment of experience. (p. 80)

This is not a diary entry, but fiction designed to impress, the parodic signalled by the deliberately over-the-top metaphor of tasting, chewing, swallowing and spitting out. But again, as in the first imagined episode, neither the dream nor the self-image can be sustained, and this is a pattern that is repeated in almost all the first person passages, a movement from comfortable fantasy to a more painful kind of "truth" and from parody to something more direct in style. Reality bites here when the woman is discovered with another lover (though this actually repeats what happened at the party in Chapter 3), and Alex is shown as being unable to sustain the idea of a character, based on himself, who can refrain from the judgemental moralism of the respectable middle classes. As the "I" acknowledges: "As it turned out, I only succeeded in making everything cheap, and silly and squalid. I suppose that's what she meant when she said I was contemptuous of her" (p. 83).The episode also connects to the epigraph from Nietzsche's *The Use and Abuse of History* in pointing to one of the illusions that Alex must shed: that even if he resigns from commitment to political activism, there can be no escape from the condition of being in history.[22]

The one occasion when the "I" of Alex's narratives portrays himself as feeling some connection to the working-class Jamaican world comes in Chapter 6 (a chapter that signals Patterson's talent for comedy) when he discovers a shared delight in the thought of imminent apocalypse, of the world (or more specifically Jamaica) being judged and wiped clean by a threatened hurricane:

> For once I can say I detect a vital unity among my people. For everyone: maidservants and their mistresses; rich men, poor men, black men, white men and most of all brown men; the dwellers of Mona Heights and the dwellers of the shanty towns – all express alike their sweet concern in their own sweet ways. There is a unity in the land at last and all men of goodwill wait with overt dismay, with covert relish, for the coming of the storm. (p. 92)

Perhaps this voice is borrowed from V.S. Reid, whose *New Day* Patterson regarded as the archetypal bourgeois Jamaican novel in its blurring of the reality of class interests in the society. Whatever, the pompous formality is not Patterson's, but the voice of someone who is taking his role as a West Indian writer, who speaks for the whole society, very seriously. But even here the universal sympathies turn out to be illusory. It is a male camaraderie in the barber's shop that turns in unkind condemnation on the young woman who dares to speak sensibly of her relief that the hurricane's threat has passed, and then the "I" breaks his moment of communion with the barber (who is taking down his protective boards), by displaying what he thinks is superior knowledge (and, of course, also referencing a state of nothingness):

> "Such a goddamn waste of time," he grumbled wearily.
> "Did you know," I offered consolingly, "that at the heart of the hurricane there is only a vacuum?"
> Without replying he walked to the back door and flung the planks away. (p. 95)

Even more deliberately mannered in style (and utterly differ-ent from the passages in *The Children of Sisyphus* that deal with the reasoning of the Rastafarians) is Chapter 7, where there is, I suspect, a parody of the biblical, Bunyonesque repetitions of initial sentence structure and phrase, the piling of adjective/noun pairings and the archaisms that one finds in the "Chorus of People in the Lane" episodes in Roger Mais's *Brother Man* (1954).[23] Here, the narrating "I" writes:

> Today I drifted to the marketplace. I wandered idly among the people. Among the screaming higglers and fat peasant women with their oily black skin who smelt of yams and cocos and coconut oil and the other things of the earth. Among the vegetables, the black-eyed peas, green bananas, sweet potatoes and trash-heaps which smelt of the sweat of the higglers and the peasant women and the other things of the earth.
>
> I rubbed shoulders with the buyers and I haggled with the sellers. There were many ladies of good breeding there, brown ladies, pink ladies and even nice black ladies, all with their haggard, reluctant housemaids struggling behind them with huge baskets filled with the fat of the land.
>
> I wandered in the noise, the great, perpetual din of the city in the marketplace. (p. 96)

This is someone from the middle class romanticising and creat-ing literary material from what he doesn't quite know ("…and the other things of the earth"). He also encounters some "cultists":

> And there were older men with beards who all stood aloof. A part of the horde, yet away from it all. These wise men spoke incessantly, and with great reverence, of another land called Ethiopia, that same place which the heathens called Africa, where all was bliss and peace and love. Where the nastiness, the greed, the suffering, the cheap, maddening indignity of the marketplace, did not exist. (p. 97)

And then the would-be novelist invents a quite deliberately absurd piece of cursing by one of the cultists, with the ludicrous image of the cold lemonade and the toe-roasting (remember, this is the same Patterson who is so accurate and insightful about the Rastafarians and their speech in *The Children of Sisyphus*):

"Thou shall burn, Babylon; oh you son of Sodom; you who was mothered in whoredom and villainy; if you are not with us, then you are against us; an' if you are against us then you shall surely suffer the dreadful fate of the oppressors. Your tongue shall be plucked out! You shall be made to thirst until the verge of death with a glass of cold lemonade dangling less than an inch from your lips. Then you shall be roasted slowly from the big toes upwards. There will be no mercy; no mercy whatever for the oppressors of the children of the black God, the children of slavery, the true Israelites!"

"Are you a Jew, then?" I asked him timidly. (p. 97)

Following the market episode, Alex's "I" visits a beach where initially he has an epiphanic, Walcottian, New-World-Adams moment[24] of a Romantic apprehension of nature (complete with pathetic fallacy), described in an over-the-top parody of the clichés of bad West Indian lyricism:

I looked over the trees and could just see the blue face of the water grinning at me through the leaves. Enticed […] I suddenly came face to face with the wide, quiet grandeur of the ocean. The confrontation was at first wonderful, overwhelming. I felt like a bedraggled Columbus: tired, lost, on the verge of giving up, suddenly seeing his new world. It was mine, this great, silent thing. I felt I was the first to see it, the first to smell it, the first to fully experience it. The eyes of others had no doubt fallen on it before. Perhaps they had even dared to bathe in it. But I, I was the first to feel it in this way. I was the first to whom it had such meaning, such sanctity. (p. 98)

But then the experience turns into a nightmare of existential dread as the character is confronted by a seascape that in its irrationality threatens his humanness and leaves him feeling "on the verge of being crushed to pulp". It's an episode that marks the beginning of the stripping back of Alex to a state of nothingness, in a way that appears to reference a passage in Frantz Fanon's *Black Skin, White Masks* (1952, 1967), where Fanon ironically re-enacts the psycho-drama of coming to terms with "The Fact of Blackness". Fanon ends the passage with these words:

Yesterday, awakening to the world, I saw the sky turn upon itself utterly and wholly. I wanted to rise, but the disembowelled

18

silence fell back upon me, its wings paralysed. Without responsibility, straddling Nothingness and Infinity, I began to weep. [25]

Alex describes his disintegration (as the "thing", "it") in the same kind of apocalyptic imagery:

> Then slowly, but with agonising certainty, the thing which faced it began to realise, however dimly, that it was being trapped. For the motion of the arcs was gathering pace till the whole universe had formed one vast gigantic circle. And it was lost there in the centre of it. (p.100)

There is a further parodic episode in Chapter 8, which follows Alex's account of his rescue by two fishermen from the collapse described above. It begins the following day with "I"/Alex leaving a brothel in the early hours of the morning, when it is impossible not to hear echoes of Aimé Césaire's great poem, *Cahier d'un retour au pays natal*. It comes in the repeated references to the time of the morning ("Au bout du petit matin" becomes in "the chill of the morning dew", "in the silence of the dawn" "the morning crept more and more upon me"); in the topography of squalid narrow streets and overcrowded houses; in the poetic prose with its repetitions, its accumulation of details and rushing cadences. For instance, when dawn breaks, "I"/Alex's sense of the dreamlike beauty of the dawn breaks too:

> But then I heard the loud, tired yawn of a whore coming from the hovels; I heard the obscene laughter of the satiated client; I heard her vile, angry retort. I walked quickly away, my hand covering my ears like a madman [...] I ran and ran between the narrow streets, bouncing between garbage men, falling over the carcases of rotting dogs, slipping on the slime of gutters and falling on my face squashed upon the asphalt. (p. 106)

This echoes a passage of Césaire's such as:

> Et cette joie ancienne m'apportant la connaissance de ma présente misère, un route bossuée qui pique une tête dans un creux où elle éparpille quelques cases: une route infatigable qui charge à fond de train du morne en haut duquel elle s'enlise brutalement dans une mare de maisons pataudes, une route follement montante, témérairement decandante, et la carcase

des bois comiquement juchée sur de minuscules pattes de ciment que j'appelle <notre maison>, sa coiffure de tôle ondulant au soleil comme une peau qui sèche...

(And this former joy brings me news of my present misery, a broken-backed street dives into a hollow where it scatters a few huts; an indefatigable road runs at full speed uphill, and is at once swallowed by a puddle of houses, a foolishly ascending, daringly descending road, and that wooden carcass, which I call <our house>, comically perched on small feet of cement, its iron coiffure corrugating in the sun like skin hung up to dry...)[26]

This is a multilayered reference that connects the returning natives of poem and novel, and engages Alex in an implicit dialogue with the ideology of Negritude and, in particular, its use of the history/myth of a glorious Negro past. In his early morning wanderings, the character "I"/Alex allows himself to be seduced into a dream where Kingston has transformed into "the relic of some ancient city", and, satirically, behind his back, the authorial voice has him wondering:

> What ancient civilisation flourished here long, long ago? How clever and resourceful they must have been to have made houses as durable as these out of the sides of empty codfish barrels. Who were the men that ruled them? Were they of another race, of another culture? How great and ingenious they must have been to create a mosaic of streets such as these. And in the same grid pattern as the Romans, too. (p. 104)

And he tries to persuade himself that:

> it is not possible, it cannot be, that all there is, that all there ever was, are the harsh sounds of the cracking of cart-whips, the vile curses of cruel, inhuman masters, the rhythm of steel hoes plunging into unyielding, virgin soil. And what have they done to my great, immortal works of art? (p. 104)

In the ironies embedded in these words, Patterson echoes Fanon when he parted company with Negritude, his condemnation in *The Wretched of the Earth* of the tendency of the intellectual petit bourgeoisie to exoticise the pre-colonial past.[27] The phrase "the rhythm of steel hoes plunging into unyielding, virgin soil" appears to reference a quotation from Césaire that Patterson uses in an highly critical essay on Negritude ("Twilight of a Dark Myth"), that he wrote in 1965. Here Patterson notes that Césaire points to the limitations of historical romanticism, in a "moving" way, when he writes:

"ma négritude n'est ni une tour ni une cathedrale

*elle plonge dans la chair rouge du sol*
elle plonge dans la chair ardente du ciel" [my italics]
[my Negritude is neither a tower nor a cathedral// it thrusts into the red flesh of the soil/it thrusts into the warm flesh of the sky][28]

However, he also argues that Césaire fails to reject the essentialism of race, and that this is the point where "Négritude reaches a dead end", because "what exactly is this black soul, this black essence?"[29] In the "petit matin" episode in *An Absence of Ruins*, "I" breaks from the delusional myth when he wakes suddenly to the sound of the waking people, but it is a present from which all possibility has gone: "They are real people; living things. True I can see their skeletons, but there is nothing of the past about their eyes. They are as of now. Everything is as of now" (p. 106). A little later, in Chapter 10, Alex makes his own decisive break with cultural nationalism when he asks, "Must I shout all that consummate shit about how they've stolen my golden Africa with its empires which they tried to cover up?" (p. 116).

The last two episodes of first person narration, in Chapters 9 and 10, take a different form from those that came before, and shape the novel's movement towards its conclusion. There's a far closer connection between the "I" and the "he", and a more plausibly diary-like form, but above all, there's a reversal of the relationship between the first and third person modes. Up to this point, the "I" narratives make fictions out of the events or situations outlined in or suggested by the third person chapters; whereas in Chapters 9 and 10, the "I" reflections generate the urge to cast aside introspection to confront the "reality" of Alex's life, with tragic-comic consequences. It as if, in the third person sections of Chapter 10, when he comically botches an attempt to drown himself, and Chapter 11, when he embarks on his farcical plan to fake his suicide (shades of *Tom Sawyer* or Preston Sturges' *Sullivan's Travels*[30]), Alex figuratively enters his own story. It is also at this point in the novel that what is genuinely moving in Alex's story and what is darkly comic begin to cross.

Up until Chapter 9, what we see of Alex is wholly his present as a middle-class intellectual who is suffering a crisis of identity and commitment. In Chapter 9, "I/Alex" begins to reflect movingly on his childhood awareness that he was making a journey away from the peasant world towards becoming an anglicised colonial, and the loss it involved. Here there are no rhetorical flourishes, but plainness and restraint. Indeed, one is tempted to feel Patterson may actually be revealing something of himself in these reflections on the letters to "Just William", the songs about Britain that could only be loved "by dissociating myself from their content" (p. 108), while "his own folk songs" he had "learned to think of as silly peasant prattle" (p. 109). Alex's reflections on his loss make him unable to ignore the relationship that condenses these divisions, that with his mother, and he rushes off to see her to declare his guilt over their separation. It is a scene that inevitably ends in "self-embarrassment at the sheer artificiality and insincerity of what he had brought himself into" (p. 112).

In this chapter, Patterson draws on Sartre's concept of bad faith to connect Alex's crisis to his unacknowledged Jamaican cultural residues. It's significant, for instance, that when Alex talks about responsibility or conscience, he invariably uses the word "guilt", and later, as the fake suicide holed up in the hills, he thinks about passing judgement and beating those who look on him "with the rod of guilt", wanting their "contrition" and himself "absolved (p. 130)". He can listen without irony to the hymn coming from the nearby peasant church: "*Are your garments spotless? Are they white as snow?*" Alex is clearly not the secular sophisticate he imagines or would have his associates think, and this gap in his self-awareness must surely be seen as contributing to his collapse.

Then in Chapter 10, after his dream of being unable to enter the room at the top of the stairs, "frozen in anguish; unable to go back, unable to go forward" – an obvious metaphor for the limbo of his position between the peasant world to which he cannot return, and the white world in which he feels he can't belong – Alex begins a Sartrean analysis of his alienation and inauthenticity ("Always I keep yearning to be what I am, but never was"

(p. 117)). He looks for excuses in race, society and history, but arrives at the Sartrean conclusion that "[t]here are no excuses to be found". Again, as in the previous chapter, the dead-end of reflection prompts him to action, also of a disastrous kind, when he hurls the diary away and embarks on his absurd and comic adventure of attempted and then faked suicide.

Yet within the absurdist farce (and the encounter with the nightwatchman is very funny) a serious question is being posed about whether, from a state of non-being (what Fanon describes in *Black Skin, White Masks*, as "an extraordinary sterile and arid region, an utterly naked declivity"), an "authentic upheaval can be born".[31] Part Three begins with the rapid discarding of the dream that running to the hills can be a return to origins, or that it is possible "[t]o become again the innocent consciousness of a child; to see the world no further up than the knees of adults..." (p. 125). This references one of the ways the Nietzsche epigraph allows a very temporary escape from history. Alex, though, rapidly casts aside the rural idyll of childhood when the "squeaking of the crickets grew irritatingly monotonous" (p. 125). But in other respects, shorn of the supports of urban familiarity, Alex does indeed revert to childishness when he asks, discovering that his "suicide" has still gone unreported, "Could it be that nobody cared?" This thought soon twists his mental contortions over the concept of responsibility into a Tom Sawyerish determination to extort guilt from those he has supposedly left behind. But when the "greatest moral battle of his life" ends in the death of his mother (an episode whose tragicomic tone achieves a Brechtian kind of distancing), Alex discovers that once he has stripped away all the inauthentic parts of his identity (of politics, race, family and marriage) in an attempt to reach a bedrock of authenticity (good faith), all that he finds is "the squalid, incongruous fool I am" (p. 140). He thinks that he has been searching for a clear vision of what he can be responsible for and the scope of his freedom. He discovers, though, that the pursuit of genuine guilt (i.e. responsibility) cannot be "the essence of my being", but only something he becomes through his actions, and thus far his actions are marked by folly.

Blackman's story ends with him as a "nowhere man", though

shorn of illusions. But does this make the novel nihilistic?

It is clear that Patterson's contemporaries were puzzled by what they took to be his vision in the novel. What *was* Patterson – the radical sociologist of slavery, the author who gave dignity to the poor in *The Children of Sisyphus*, the Fanonian, the contributor to *New Left Review* – doing by writing a novel that appeared to ally him with the "reactionary" V.S. Naipaul of "Nothing was created in the Caribbean" or the Walcott who was seen as pursuing a Eurocentric humanism at a time when writers were meant to be recovering the folk and Africa in the Caribbean?

I'd argue that in writing *An Absence of Ruins* Patterson was being true to the questioning spirit of Fanon, and that the kind of class-analysis of the New Left Marxism that Patterson espoused in that period was not incompatible with appreciating the rigorous honesty of V.S. Naipaul's work as expressed in, for instance, *The Mimic Men*, published in the same year.[32] Further, Patterson uses two key epigraphs by Dostoyevsky and Walcott which qualify Alex's apparent dead-end as the wandering ghostly figure in London.

The Dostoyevsky epigraph connects its unnamed narrator's constant state of taunted restlessness to Alex's situation. The unnamed Russian can only offer himself a "useless consolation" in the act of withdrawal, because the option of doing nothing is just as impossible as engaging in action. In the same way, Alex is condemned to "keep up the appearance of going in order to forget that I am not." But his desire for invisibility is evidently not one he can realise any more than the unnamed man can find consolation, since we see Alex being trapped by a real native of the city and confronted with his anomalous savage/civilised status. Because of how Alex looks, this is a question that won't go away; perhaps we are meant to see it as the grit that will drive Alex at some point to deconstruct the dichotomy in which the native of London wants to trap him. In the meantime, Alex's final statement is both evasive and utopian. As a human being, he cannot stand, as he claims, "outside race, outside of culture, outside of history, outside of any value that could make your question meaningful" (p. 146). It's an ending which makes, perhaps, the last parodic, intertextual reference in the novel: to Denis William's *Other Leopards* (1963) with its anti-hero, perched in a tree and declaring, "I am without context".[33] But Alex's statement is also utopian in the sense that, only a few years later, Patterson was to argue that, without denying the reality of racial oppression, Black Americans faced a historic choice, "an awesome opportunity". This was to accept the challenge of being the "first group in the history of mankind who transcend the confines and grip of a cultural heritage, and in so doing, they can become the most truly modern of all peoples – a people who feel no need for a nation, a past, or a particularistic culture…"[34] Now clearly this reflection is not part of the novel and was written a few years after it, but it fits with Patterson's consistent hostility to cultural nationalism and the politics of ethnic identity, and as such it suggests that the meaning of Alex's fate is more complex than it appears. He is clearly in a "sterile and arid region", but whether it is one from which, to quote Fanon, "an authentic upheaval can be born", the reader is left to imagine.

I think, too, that we are intended to see Alex's particular failure within the more positive context of the vision implicit in the epigraph drawn from Walcott's poem, "The Royal Palms… an absence of ruins", which Patterson no doubt uses to qualify the negativity of the Naipaul edict to which the novel's title inevitably points. Walcott's poem challenges Naipaul's reading of the Caribbean as having created nothing, by countering the literal and figurative monumental legacies of imperial European history with an image of a different kind of human creativity:

> You will not find in these green, desert places
> One stone that found us worthy of its name,
> Nor how, lacking the skill to beat things over flame,
> We peopled archipelagoes by one star.[35]

The other point to be made about Alex's trajectory is that it is not the only one in the novel (and there's an interesting parallel here with Garth St. Omer's *A Room on the Hill* (1967)[36]). To charge *An Absence of Ruins* with negativity and nihilism is to ignore the fact that, if Alex moves towards nullity in his attempt to escape from his mother and his conflicted situation as a Jamaican, his abandoned wife, Pauline, moves from a state of humiliating dependence on Alex to a position of self-awareness (on which she acts) and confident independence (even if this does involve the predatory sympathy of Alex's friend, Edward). There is the other opening epigraph too – Bessie Smith's line, "See that long lonesome road? Don't you know it's got an end?" – and the connection to Alex's mother, "a tall stout, dark-brown woman… who looked remarkably like Bessie Smith" (p. 45). If the middle-class male intellectuals are making a mess of things in the novel, perhaps hope for the future lies with women.

## NOTES

1. It satirised members of the New World Group such as Lloyd Best, and the character of John Fitzmaurice probably contains a dash of John Hearne.
2. See for instance Kamau Brathwaite, *LX: The Love Axe/l*, Vol. 1 (Leeds: Peepal Tree Press, 2012), pp. 89, 105. The judgement dates from the 1970s.
3. Bridget Jones, "Some French Influences in the Fiction of Orlando Patterson", *Savacou*, 11/12 (1975), 27-38.
4. Jones, "Some French Influences", p. 38
5. John Hearne, "The Novel as Sociology as Bore", *Caribbean Quarterly*, Vol. 18, No. 4 (December 1972), 78-81.
6. Lamming, *The Pleasures of Exile* (London: Michael Joseph, 1960), pp. 48-52. In "Outside History: Jamaica Today", Patterson writes of the rural working classes as being trapped in a world that had little changed since emancipation, so that "On the gaunt, suspicious faces of the rural masses the marks of a whole history of social chaos, of economic and political tyranny are visible".
7. See for instance, Anne Walmsley, *The Caribbean Artists Movement, 1966-1972* (London: New Beacon Books, 1992), pp. 52, 66-67.
8. Introduction to *The Children of Sisyphus* (Leeds: Peepal Tree Press, 2012), p. 19.
9. "Some French Influences…", p. 28.
10. For Rodney's view see <http://www.solidarity-us.org/node/136>. However, it should not be assumed that Patterson favoured Rodney's position, which he saw as being black culturalist.
11. See *Season of Adventure* (London: Michael Joseph, 1960), pp. 330-332; and see Bill Schwartz, "C. L. R. James and George Lamming: The Measure of Historical Time", *Small Axe*, No. 14, (Vol. 7, No. 2, September 2003), 39-70.

12. R.D. Laing, *The Politics of Experience & The Bird of Paradise* (London: Penguin, 1967), p. 16.
13. *The Children of Sisyphus* (Leeds: Peepal Tree Press, 2012), pp. 121, 125-126.
14. "Blacks in the Americas", *Savacou*, 9/10 (1974), 112-119.
15. "Outside History: Jamaica Today", *New Left Review*, 1/31, May-June 1965. Available on-line, no pagination.
16. "Outside History". Patterson was sceptical because of the tribalism of Jamaican politics, the control of the so-called mass parties by the middle classes, and his view that what "is vulgarly known as Jamaica's nationalist movement" hid the reality of the UK's desire to transfer political power because there had long since been no economic benefits in retaining imperial control.
17. "Outside History: Jamaica Today".
18. Jones, "Some French Influences", p. 34.
19. See Boyd Tonkin, "Two big small islands make time for jubilation: different sides of a shared story", *The Independent* (9 June 2012), p. 33.
20. See Jeremy Poynting, "Introduction" to George Lamming, *Of Age and Innocence*, (Leeds: Peepal Tree Press, 2011, pp. 15-16.
21. *The Land of the Living* (London: Faber, 1961), p. 236.
22. Nietzsche's essay goes on to explore a range of possible relations, necessary, productive or self-destructive, between contemporary societies and constructions of their pasts, asserting that whilst a consciousness of history is part of the definition of being human, particular kinds of relationship to history can damage life and choices in the present. For instance, he talks about the monumental where the weight of history leads to pessimism about present possibility.
23. See *Brother Man* (London: Cape, 1953), pp. 7-9, 59-60, 105-107.
24. See "…our profane Genesis/ whose Adam speaks that prose/ which, blessing some sea-rock, startles itself/ with poetry's surprise" in "Crusoe's Journal", *The Castaway*, 1965, p. 51.
25. Frantz Fanon, *Black Skin, White Masks* (London: MacGibbon & Kee, 1967), p. 140. Translation by Charles Lam Markmann from *Peau noire, masques blancs* (1952).
26. Aimé Césaire, *Cahier d'un retour au pays natal (Return to My Native Land)* (Paris: Présence Africaine, 1960, 1968), pp. 22-23. Translation by Emile Snyders from the 1968 dual language edition.
27. See the chapter, "On National Culture", in Fanon, *The Wretched of the Earth* (London: Penguin ed, 1965), pp. 166-199.
28. *Cahier d'un retour au pays natal*, pp. 100-101.
29. "Twilight of a Dark Myth", *TLS*, No. 3316 (16 September 1965), p. 805. In this essay, Patterson characterises Negritude as a "fossilized complex of hackneyed, rather trite evocations of atavistic senti-

ments loosely bound together by a vaguely defined central theme which very often seems little removed from outright racism".

30. There's the episode in *Tom Sawyer* where Tom imagines himself drowned and enjoys the idea of Aunt Polly's guilt for "mistreating" him, and the later scene where Tom and Huck are thought drowned, and Tom is much more excited about the idea of reappearing at his funeral than having any concern for the grief he has caused his relatives. In Preston Sturges' great film *Sullivan's Travels* (1941), the filmstar hero's attempt to discover the truth about the lives of the poor goes wildly awry when his boots are stolen by a tramp who is subsequently killed by a train and the identities of the two are thereafter switched to disastrously comic effect.

31. Fanon, *Black Skin, White Masks*, p. 10.

32. Unlike some of his colleagues in CAM, Patterson was much readier to see Naipaul's work as an honest perception of the region's problems – though he also hints at Naipaul's tendency to pathologise Caribbean societies and people in describing his work as "obsessive".

33. See *Other Leopards* (London: New Authors, 1963), quotations from the Peepal Tree Caribbean Modern Classics edition, 2009, p. 214.

34. "Toward a future that has no past – reflections on Blacks in the Americas", *The Public Interest*, No. 27 (NY,1972), pp. 60-61.

35. Derek Walcott, "The Royal Palms… an absence of ruins"; this poem was originally published in *The London Magazine*, 1, No. 11 (1962): 12–13, and only ever republished in *Negro Verse*, ed. Anselm Hollo (London: Vista Books, 1964), pp. 16-17. Patterson seems to have shared at least that part of Walcott's vision that saw the Caribbean as a place that had to be and could be made anew (see "The Muse of History"), and with Walcott's rejection of the mythologising, backwards look – though no doubt not with the mulatto culturalism implicit in Walcott's vision, which Patterson, fierce critic of all forms of ethnocentricity, would have seen as another bogus essentialism.

36. In my introduction to Garth St. Omer's *A Room on the Hill* (Leeds: Peepal Tree Press, 2011), pp. 19-21, I argue that the verdict of negativity made on that novel depends on ignoring the role of a significant woman character.

Here there are no heroic palaces
Netted in sea-green vines, or built
On maize savannahs the cat-thighed, stony faces
Of Egypt's cradle, easily unriddled;
If art is where the greatest ruins are,
Our art is in those ruins we became,
You will not find in these green, desert places
One stone that found us worthy of its name,
Nor how, lacking the skill to beat things over flame,
We peopled archipelagoes by one star.

DEREK WALCOTT: *The Royal Palms*


See that long lonesome road? Don't you know
it's got an end?

BESSIE SMITH : *Young Woman Blues*

For Rhiannon, Barbara & Kaia

# CONTENTS

# PART ONE

## CONSIDER, THE BEAST

The beast lives *unhistorically*; for it 'goes into' the present, like a number, without leaving any curious remainder. It cannot dissimulate, it conceals nothing; at every moment it seems what it actually is, and thus can be nothing that is not honest. But man is always resisting the great and continually increasing weight of the past... And so it hurts him, like the thought of a lost paradise, to see a herd grazing, or, nearer still, a child that has nothing yet of the past to disown and plays in a happy blindness between the walls of the past and the future.

F. NIETZSCHE: *The Use and Abuse of History*

# 1

...outside I stood for a while with my forehead pressing on my arm which was creased against the trunk of the mango tree. Vacantly, I stared down at the roots of the tree. It had been a dry, harsh August. The grass in the garden had withered away. The earth was parched and cracked. Stiff, dead leaves lay about, brown as the earth and motionless. The roots of the tree, though hoary, appeared strong and secure, as if they were fixed there for eternity. I turned my stare from the roots to the dry patch of land that was once a green lawn.

With that I felt more familiar. The harsh, brown, dusty aridity of everything there seems to meet some vague yet deeply embedded demand in me. It was with difficulty that I prevented myself from falling to the ground and wallowing all over in it. Little dry lot of land hemmed in by the thorny hedges, I thought to myself with tenderness. Somehow I seem to have found a momentary security there – there, in the bare, dry nakedness of everything. A security I never felt in the smug little green garden my mother kept when it was cooler. Everything was now stripped, shameless and undemanding. I faced in the barrenness the compulsive simplicity of cruelty. Above me the searing hot sun shining through a sky which was horrifying in its stark, blue clarity. Below me the earth – arid, severe and tough. I loved them. I was obsessed with them even if they inspired nothing but the desire to escape them.

I thought then that I would walk to the sea. I was sure, at that moment, that what I needed most was to linger by the edges of the ocean, to stare at the long wrinkles of the vast blue-grey blanket of the harbour. Perhaps the raw, salty sprays will touch me as the tide begins to change later in the afternoon.

Abruptly, the road ends on the seaside. There I was, confronted with the vast liquid expanse I knew I loved so much. For the sea is the only place I know in the face of which I can be absolutely certain that I will not think of it. Its essence is a separateness which at least ensures the possibility of other things. There I can dream and lust and search eternally.

So for the rest of the afternoon, perched upon the iron railing where the road ends and the sea begins, I lost count of consciousness. I became a vacancy. That point where I was sure the bluish grey of the sea met the green-blue of the sky. I can only conceive of what I was then in retrospect. The most I can say is that I was somehow lost in the oblivion of my being. Nothing more positive; certainly not whether I enjoyed it or not. I was simply there. A crude animal thing, outside of time, outside of history, outside of the consciousness of other beings. I was just there. Yet, I was enough of being just there to be aware that I had merged into everything. It was like drowning in a dream. A wonderful transient intimation of the silence of things. I was all sensation, all being; yet there is nothing in particular I can recall sensing; nor any state of mind I was aware of.

Night came down. Lights twinkle in the semicircle of the harbour. A plane glides gently in and I wonder for a moment what went on in the airport on the palisade across the harbour. Then I was conscious of the sea again. Immediately I wished to depart. Always it is like this. I can sit lost by the sea for hours, but the moment I am aware that it is there before me there is the compulsion to leave, to be somewhere else, not because I have suddenly come to loathe the sight of it, but because I need to be with it so much.

And for me to need is somehow to fear. To fear what, I am not sure. Perhaps that I shall lose. Separation must be caught before it catches up with me. I must leave the sea because I want to desire the smell of salt in the air, the teasing menace of the slightly changing tide, the gentle touch of silver sprays. To desire them I must want them; to want them I must be away from them. Confrontation terrifies me with the fear of the failure of experience. So I must escape from what I anticipate at once. Move far away, wander on the streets. Besides, I was feeling thirsty…

Soon I was on the Windward Road. As I walked I kept remembering all the advertisements for Red-Stripe beer. I believed it all now. Anything that would fill, if even momentarily, the vacancy within me; anything that would end the crippling sense of indecision that was becoming increasingly unbearable. And why not a Red-Stripe beer? They said on the radio that it was a man's drink. I knew at least that I was a man – so there, that was something meant for me. They also said that nothing could better quench your thirst. I was very thirsty – therefore I could at least decide to drink some beer. By the time I reached the rum-bar at the corner I had developed what I was sure was an insatiable need for Red-Stripe beer. I ran inside, slammed down a coin on the counter and shouted for a bottle.

I watched the barmaid intently as she took the bottle from the icebox. My mouth watered with expectancy as I saw the stopper fall away and the beautiful froth rushed joyfully to the top of the bottle. I would be satisfied, at last. In that moment, between taking the bottle from the barmaid and putting it to my lips, I experienced once more the mocking, transient hint of fulfilment which nibbled furtively at me from time to time. Then, expectation became reality. Everything I wanted was now reduced to the simple, trite desire for my thirst to be quenched. In that instant, it would seem, I was a man of faith once again. I knew what I wanted and I knew how it should be attained. Must I be blamed for waiting so long before actually drinking?

But the moment had to come. The first time I swallowed I was still too overwhelmed with expectation to appreciate its realisation. The second time I already began to sense an anticlimax. By the third I was disappointed: the fourth disgusted me. And the fifth I spat out in revulsion.

I heard the barmaid scream and move away; but she was too late, for the beer had caught one end of her skirt.

'You dirty little rass-hole!' she swore, running towards the till. From behind it she took a long butcher's knife and came towards me. The drunks in the bar began to look round as she bellowed out what I had done. She ran to the other end of the counter, looking at me all the time with a glint of wickedness in her eyes. I kept my seat calmly and waited for her.

She charged up to within a few inches of me, then stopped suddenly. She was a stout, black woman with smooth, oily skin which was overcoated with white powder. Her large brown eyes bulged and glared and her cheeks puffed out as she panted in rage at me. I held my peace. A look of surprise gradually overcame her. She seemed thoroughly disappointed that I had not run away, as it had robbed her of the opportunity of chasing after me with threats of murder. I know, after what had happened, it was a matter of simple courtesy to at least have pretended that she had the right to expect that I feared she would have murdered me. But I was in no mood to be polite and continued to stare at her imperturbably. She looked at the knife in her hand and I could see she felt silly. 'You dirty dog!' she said, very unconvincingly, and walked back to the other side of the counter. I got up and left.

The air outside was warm and clammy. People passed me by on the narrow street. Like ants. Except they seemed to lack any sense of purpose. On the faces of a few there was a kind of anticipation; or perhaps it was a look of earnestness, especially the Revivalists dressed in their white satin dresses with the pious, long sleeves. But they, after all, were the few who had completely opted out. They had resigned themselves to prolonging their existence till sweet Jesus was ready for them. And until then they would pray to be saved from his wrath.

The rest, the multitude, who had remained earthbound, committed to their earthly existence simply by default, seem to have long given up the idea of going anywhere. They lingered in little groups on the corners listening to the jukeboxes, shouting, laughing, jeering, forever dawdling. Often, to break the monotony, there was the affectation of anger and someone would pull a knife or dash for a broken bottle. But no one took him seriously. Anger had long become a tired joke; an emotion to be played at, and hardly worth a giggle. They simply lingered and waited for nothing. And when they were bored with lingering they danced to the rhythm of the ska.

For the ska was free. And it was everywhere – a harsh, pulsatile ubiquitous ode to monotony. Nothing escaped the cynicism of its lyrics: there were ballads of love, tales of pain in the belly, quotations from the Bible incoherently pieced together; there were folksongs, nursery rhymes and hymns, unearthly tales of Jezebels and humpty-dumpties. They were all sung to the same beat, listened to with the same easy humour of the cynical, danced to with the same meaningless contortions of abandonment.

I passed them without looking at them. For they all wore the same mask. They were all painted with the dazed, subdued astonishment of the lost. Besides, I did not care to see them. Why should I? I, of all persons, so very much one of them.

I walked slowly, aimlessly, past the brothels of the Mountain View Road. I began to feel I wanted to urinate and was glad for something to do, to look forward to. I held back as long as possible, relishing the expectation of relief. Carefully, I chose my spot – a dark, narrow passage beside a cold-supper shop. As I eased myself I heard a rumble in the thrash by the hedge, looked round and saw a couple copulating. They may have seen me; they may have heard me. But they continued and I left them to their peace.

I entered the next brothel I reached. Like most in this part of the city it was situated some way in from the road, almost lost in darkness except for two strings of subdued red and green lights arranged in a cross on the mango tree that hung over it. The place was an old bungalow called The Hermitage. I had been there several times before when a student at the university. What used to be the living room had been converted into a dance hall and the music was supplied by a jukebox in one corner.

It was midweek and business was obviously slow. A few couples sat outside on the veranda. In the hall several of the whores were doing the ska among themselves. They were all slender, with terse, glowing skin, moist with sweat, except for an enormously fat one who sat sleepily in an armchair eyeing them with sneaky, half-opened eyes and who, I remember, was called Tiny.

They pretended not to see me when I entered and continued dancing, their bodies bent from the waist, their torsos bobbing up and down in an agile, repetitive bowing: necks stretching in and out like irate turkeys, hands alternating between their thighs and their chins like panting long-distance runners. Yet, despite the awkward angularity of their movements, despite the appearance of an excessive display of energy, an innate sense of rhythm

41

seemed to smooth over everything making the dance something beautiful to watch. Its vulgarity mocking itself, this ska, a droll, defiant beautification of clumsiness.

I knew they were all aware of my presence. But it was not the done thing for any of them to pounce on me too greedily. I had gone through this ritual several times before and I knew the first move depended on me. The last thing I could do was to select the woman of my choice and approach her directly. Such brashness could always be forgiven in a sailor or foreigner. But I was obviously a native and since I had no intention of being dismissed as a hurry-come-up liberty-taking bastard – a humiliation I had experienced on several occasions in my early student days – I bided my time. They were like Japanese businessmen, these whores.

I lit a cigarette and sat down looking at them. One by one their eyes caught mine. I returned the smile of those I favoured. The rest I cut dead. The disfavoured gradually melted away, most discreetly, but a few only after a nasty hiss of the teeth. The remaining three continued to dance a little longer until the record stopped playing. Then they dispersed. One went to the door nearest to me and pretended to be looking outside. The other went across to Tiny and began to tease her, looking at me out of the corner of her eyes to see if I was laughing too. The third went to the little bar in the next room and began talking to the barmaid.

It was my move again. I finished my cigarette and walked over to the girl at the counter.

'Hi!' I began.

She turned her head casually towards me, then stared at my face through glazed slanted eyes. She had strikingly curious features which were individually odd, almost grotesque, but collectively fascinating. Her face had a clearly defined Mongoloid bone structure over which the darkish yellow skin was wrapped tightly. The slanted eyes were deep, brown and cruel. The nose was an exotic compromise between Negroid prominence and Chinese delicacy – flat, pert, with two little nostrils. Her lips were unexpectedly full, almost thick. She kept wetting them with her saliva in the manner of some self-conscious Negroes, so that they were wet, cold, offensive, yet ambiguously appealing.

'Can I buy you a drink?'

'If you want,' she eventually condescended.

I got rum and water for myself and grape-juice for her.

'Ah sure that Ah see you here before,' she said, warming up.

'Yes; I used to come here when I was a student.'

Then she told me how silly she found the students these days. I agreed wholeheartedly with her and we continued in a friendly manner for the next half-hour.

My desire for her grew as we bantered on. I suppose it was the sheer vulgarity of her which was attracting me. She sat down in front of me in a perfectly relaxed fashion, her hands dangling behind the chair, her legs apart with her tight dress halfway up her thighs. Again there was that eager, surging experience of expectancy. The same I had before reaching the sea; before drinking the beer; before urinating. It was a kind of rush into emptiness; yet the very rush, the very surge, was itself an emptiness. Not for one moment really did I fool myself into believing its fulfilment would fill the indefinable cavity inside of me. These desires of mine, these sudden, trite obsessions, I knew them for what they were – little dead-ends, mirages in the desert, pauses and commas in the endless statement of my underlying hunger, itself a vacancy.

Nor were they pauses of relief, but of derision. Squalid little expectations which ended in themselves, denied of all negation, of all fulfilment. Perhaps they are my real grief, my only grief. Vacancy, after all, is only an assumption; perhaps an invention of my pride to make me more human by making my grief more difficult. Perhaps all that exists are these sordid little pauses, the pretension of vacancy being simply the illusion of what lay between them. Perhaps I search after nothing more petty than an overcoming of the fear of fully confronting a salty expanse of water, the satisfaction of a bottle of beer, the copulation with a whore...

'There is a room free now,' I heard her saying.

'Oh, is there? Well, shall we do business then?'

We got up, and she led me to a room at the back of the house. It was small, bare and there was the odour of cheap soap and water.

''Ow you takin' it,' she asked as she began undressing, 'short-time or long-time?'

'Short-time,' I said meekly, feeling silly at my slight embarrassment. The next instant I was devouring her nakedness. Where the sun had not caught her she was a bright yellow; her limbs were long and lithe, but the flesh around her belly was flaccid and curved in large wrinkles, as if she had given birth recently. The tuft of pubic hair, jumbled, grizzly and half-shaved, seemed a little grotesque on her. I suppressed a slight tinge of revulsion and encouraged my desire for her.

I took off my clothes. She stared down at me and smiled a little. I suppose it was meant to be encouraging, but I suspected that there was something not a little patronising about her expression. Then she held out her hand and asked for her money. I gave her fifty shillings. She shook her head and informed me that the cost of living had increased since I last came. I gave her another ten shillings and she put it away with a shrug. She was about to climb on the bed when she suddenly paused and said : 'Oh, by the way, the room; it cost a pound: you better make me pay it for you.'

'But I thought it was included...' but I thought better of arguing and gave her another pound, the last I had. She climbed into the bed and lay on her back and, with her arm curled around the back of her neck, she stared musingly at me. I stood by the bed, staring over every inch of her. I felt that I wanted her. I felt that I want her. Yet I remained limp and unexcited.

She stretched out her left hand and fondled me crudely as I began to climb on the bed. As my thighs touched hers and the smell of her skin filled my nostrils a surge of expectancy filled my stomach and rose through me. I became choked with the thought of the snaky movement of her body. My fingers squeezed into her breasts and she moved away.

She moved her legs apart and pulled me down on her. Now. I would fulfil the expectancy of satiating my passion for her. It was not so much that I had suddenly desired her but that I felt duty-bound to want her. I snatched at every motivation. My four pounds; my masculine pride; my desire to hurt her; my revulsion.

But I remained limp, unmoved, frozen in expectancy. She was there under me, I forced myself to believe, to understand – a woman, a whore, a beast with two legs, two arms, two breasts, a womb that opened out into tissues of voluptuousness. There for the taking. But what was she? Despite her nearness I felt then that I was incapable of knowing. What is more, I hardly cared. I could not have cared, for in that moment everything that she was, everything about her that should excite me, that should make her a living thing, a woman to mate with, was caught up on the intensity of my expectancy for her. She, whatever she was, existed as a real thing only in the anticipation of my total confrontation with her. And in that there was only fear, only the choking sensation of anxiety, only the compulsion to escape fulfilment and to plunge into the swampy engulfment of further anticipation.

Suddenly I felt sick. I snatched myself out of the bed and...

'Richard!' he heard his mother calling.

'Yes!' he answered impatiently.

'Darling, it is time for you to get some sleep.'

He looked round and saw her standing at the door. She was a tall, stout, dark-brown woman with short hair who looked remarkably like Bessie Smith. Her expression was kind, concerned and slightly curious as she looked at him.

'I'll soon turn in, Mam; honestly, I just want to finish this thing...'

'Is it your diary?'

'Yes.'

'Seems more like a book you're writing. But you must get some sleep, dear. I didn't like the way you looked when you came in tonight. My God, I had the shock of my life; you looked so exhausted and weak; I'm sure there's something wrong...'

'Oh for heaven's sake, Mam, I told you I was just a little tired; that's all; I'm perfectly all right.'

'Yes, but you still promise you'll go and see the doctor?'

'For your sake, yes...'

He took up his pen and pretended to be writing in his diary again, hoping that she would leave. But she persisted. He glanced around at her and recognised that benign look of inquiry which he knew meant that she would not be leaving until she had been satisfied about what she wanted to know. She walked towards him slowly and slightly apologetically, but this was more in the manner of saying she was sorry for disturbing him. She was a very determined person.

He closed the diary and placed it at the other end of the table.

She came up close to him and rubbed her palm over his head. He stared away and sighed a little by way of responding to her warmth.

'What is the matter, dear? Is it Pauline?'

'Nothing is the matter, for the hundredth time. And if there was why should it be Pauline anyway?'

'When are you going to see her again?'

'Tomorrow I guess.'

'And what's going to happen?'

'Oh, I'll just end the whole thing once and for all. I'll take my things and leave. This time it will be the end.'

'You sure that's what you want to do?'

'Oh, don't be silly, Mam, of course that's what I want to do. Can you see any other alternative. I've left her and gone back three times. It's becoming absurd. I'm through with it.'

'But why do you keep going back, son? Each time you say the same thing, yet you go back.'

'It's hard to say. I suppose I felt too committed to her… it's guilt, largely. Nobody realises as much as I do just how much I've hurt her. I kept telling myself that we had to hit it off somehow. I forced myself to love her. I was such a fool. But now I'm through.'

'You sure?'

'What do you mean? Of course I'm sure.'

'Yet even since you left the last time you've still been seeing her. You feel so sure you're through with her and yet less than two weeks after walking out on her you went back again.'

'Who told you that? Oh, I wish she didn't have to act as if you are my keeper. Why must she come to you with…?'

'You never mind that. But don't you think you should make up your mind once and for all. Your indecision is what is hurting her most, you know.'

'I know, I know! It's this damn' little island. How can I help bumping into her? What is there to do except to see her? I'm getting out. The sooner I leave the better.'

'You born here and grow up here. You belong here. It's your home.'

'Oh, Mam, you should know better than to talk like that. You, of all people. Who curses this place more than you? You're hardly back a month from New York and you want to go back on vacation again.'

'It's not a vacation. It's work. I don't have any alternative.'

'Don't give me that, Mam. Between what I give you and what you earn from the shop you can more than make ends meet here, hard as it is. Yet the first opportunity you get you're off on one of those working vacations of yours. I have a good mind to report you to the American Consul.'

'Yes,' she said smilingly, 'but when I'm in New York I do want to come back. I feel I belong here.'

'That's only nostalgia; it's one of the most frivolous and empty of emotions. I felt the same in London sometimes. But you only have to be back here a few days before you want to leave again. It's all so barren, so claustrophobic.'

'Where do you intend to go then?'

'I don't know, back to London; New York perhaps...'

'I thought you hated those cities.'

'I still do. But there is at least something challenging in hating your environment. What's more, there is no compulsion to feel you ought to belong there. You know you're rejected, so there's no threat of being swallowed up. You know perfectly well where you stand – on the fringes; and I like that; you can't imagine how undemanding it can be.'

'I don't understand you; Lord you worry me so.'

Her voice had a mild crack of grief. The fact that she no longer knew him filled her momentarily with fear. The fear of realising the stark truth that she had lost him. There he was before her: thirty years of effort, of sacrifice, of pain, of ambition, the fulfilment of all which was this person, this stranger whom she was incapable of understanding, of sympathising with. He had cut himself off, the distorted shadow, the living ghost of the thing she had created and cherished and loved. Now all the wide, intense warmth of her love could not succeed in melting even a drop of feeling, with which she could feel familiar, from the solid brick of ice that his being had frozen into.

'You're so different,' she said sadly, softly, for she preferred to weep to herself. 'Ever since you came back you've been so different. I don't know what they did to you across there, but you've changed; changed. You seem plagued with some evil spirit. Something always seems on your mind. You're here but you're never here. I hardly know you anymore, my own son.'

He sighed impatiently.

'Please, Mam, not again…'

'All right, all right; I'm going,' she said, heaving a deep sigh; then she added defiantly: 'But whatever you are, you still remain my son. Don't you forget. I'm going to pray hard for you.'

She caressed the back of his neck as he stared blankly at the wall in front of him; then slowly she left the room. He snatched his diary hurriedly, took up his pen, but as he placed it on the paper all his thoughts seemed to dry up. He closed the book once more and flung it to the other end of the table. It was a pity about the way his mother felt, he thought. Perhaps he should have said something consoling. Oh but he hated being sentimental. Besides, he propitiated himself, she was a tough woman.

He got up, stretched, and changed into his pyjamas. But it was too hot and he immediately took them off. Then he slumped into bed, naked. As he lay there, his head crushed into the pillow, each little incident of the day that had passed came back to him. They came incoherently, in brief, distorted flashes, as if in a dream, although he remained wide awake. Though vague in form each incident had the same biting impact. They came back like a school of fish, each picking away at his helpless body floating in a vast swamp of morass and dark, murky water, then darting away, and coming back, teasingly picking, picking, picking till he was only a floating skeleton with two enormous, slimy eyes that possessed a consciousness of their own, making him aware of what he was, where he was, what was happening to him…

He was floating in a swamp, but it was the sea none the less. It was black and murky, but he could see clearly through it. Huge gulps of water passed through him. The waves broke into froths of beer; he could smell it, he could just about taste it, but when he swallowed he felt or tasted nothing, for it fell away through his ribs and returned to the dark, mucous liquid of the ocean. And the undulations of the waves were the folds of her belly. He floated up and down with the copulative movements of the water. He drank it and he could taste it now and his body could hold it now, for the fish had gone away and his bones were clothed with flesh again. But now it was only froth and as it reached his throat each of the million little bubbles burst and tickled him and he could hear the laughter of the water everywhere…

He saw her now, live and real, far, far more real than he had thought it possible before. She had her right arm still placed nonchalantly behind her neck; and her left hand was still fondling him crudely. 'You paid your money,' he heard her saying, 'why don't you take me?' Then he sunk into her. Into the swamp. Into the morass. Into the ocean of abyss. He felt the waves of her belly pounding him expertly; he heard the crude moan of her affected delight, flattering his masculinity. And he sunk deeper and deeper into her until he crashed hard upon the rocks of the bottom of the dark ocean which were covered over with lurid, transparent slime…

Suddenly he snatched himself out of the bed, shocked. His body was swamped with sweat. The sheet was wet and soppy. Still panting, he stared in disbelief at the pool of semen. He swore aloud, went for the towel, and wiped himself. Then he changed the sheet and lay down again, this time on his back. He lit a cigarette and stared vacantly at the smoke as it mushroomed towards the ceiling and faded in the dry, harsh silence. In the other room he could hear the mumble of his mother as she prayed.

# 2

...furthermore, he continued, he had married her out of pure selfishness. There had been no love. Not even any real desire. She must have known it. How could she have been so insensitive as not to have realised it? It had been solely a matter of not wanting anyone else to have her. It was no use arguing. No use telling him how she thought he felt. He was quite certain he did not love her, that he never did.

'But how can you say that? How can you ?' Her voice had the pleading, hopelessly confused tone that irritated him. There was something helplessly feminine about it that made him flush with embarrassment for her and at the same time excited in him a strange, criminal desire to hurt her physically. He became guilty at the ghastliness of his feelings and tried to rid himself of them by trying to conceive of how Elaine would have responded in the same situation. Elaine. She was so strong. So composed. It was impossible even to conceive of her in such a situation. She was everything that...

'You're not listening to me,' she pleaded, 'at least you can do me the favour of listening to what I have to say.' In her voice now was the mildest attempt at protest. The little boy was angry with the weak young dog. He slashed its hide over and over again with the tamarind switch. At last, unable to run, it gives one defiant squeak. And how enraged the boy was. What insolence. In an instant there was the cruel urge to bash its head in.

Once more the incredible meanness of his feelings drove him to guilt. His guilt only intensified his anger at her. His mouth dropped open. He turned away and his hand touched her naked hips accidentally. Immediately something in him recoiled in a chill of revulsion. He sought to salve his conscience by deliberately caressing the loose skin of her rib. The deliberateness of the act made it artificial to the point of embarrassment.

He moved his hand away quickly when he realised he was hurting her. Yet she had not complained. The cruel, unthinking crease of his fingernails was still there in her skin; and it had not even occurred to her to make the slightest sign of protest. Had she convinced herself that she had enjoyed it? What kind of person was she? What had her feelings for him made of her?

'Please, at least listen to what I have to say,' she was repeating. Now there was not the slightest note of protest in her voice. She was begging. Now nothing, absolutely nothing, was left with which he could placate his guilt for her. She had robbed him even of that. She had given herself up completely to his mercy and had left him bare, contrite, exposed to himself.

His guilt confronted him pure and inexcusable. Once more he was overwhelmed by the sordidness of his emotions, by the strength of his desire to be guiltless in the face of the soul-consuming intensity of his guilt. His fingers splashed across his face, one of his thumbs piercing his lips senselessly. There was a strange taste of bitterness in his mouth. He swallowed hard.

'Oh Christ almighty,' he sighed heavily in despair. Then he remembered she had been trying to say something.

'What is it?'

She made no reply.

'Well, what is it you were saying?'

'Nothing.'

Her meekness shocked him. It was not her. He had bludgeoned her into this. She used to be a thing of passion – conscious, responsive, utterly alive. What was she now?

He sought desperately to resurrect the almost dead thing of her soul. He had to make her speak; to bring back the life in her. It was his responsibility, his guilt.

'What is it, darling? For God's sake, what is it?'

His voice trembled with anger, much against his will. He realised full well that forcing her to speak only crippled her more. But she had to speak. Her silence was agony. Every moment that it lasted measured out the extent of his cruelty. He was hurting her. Little by little he was stifling her, killing her.

The strange subdued shaft of moonlight; the limp, shaded curtains; the long, drooped silhouettes of coconut palms; the shadowy, half-suggested form of the furniture; and the dull glow of her naked body – they were all one in the semidarkness of the evening. And they were all shocked in a disbelieving silence, confounded by his cruelty.

'Pauline, please…' he said.

'It's not important,' she replied.

Her voice had regained some of its life. It contained something of anger mingled with a determination to say nothing, which relieved him a little inasmuch as it made it possible for him to be annoyed with some justification. He controlled himself and pleaded once more, this time, to his own surprise, with some sincerity – perhaps because now there was some genuine curiosity about what she had to say – and managed to put his hand round her back with an affectation of tenderness.

She cleared her throat and he waited impatiently as she fidgeted back into a mood of communication.

'Well…'

She paused, and he just managed to prevent an angry exclamation of 'Well what?' But he was hopeless at disguising his feelings. She detected his impatience and slumped back into her despair.

The silence that followed was long, intense and cruel. There was only the paralysing consciousness of each other; the desire to negate that consciousness by communication; and the consciousness of the inability to communicate. It was like slowly dying of suffocation in a vacuum. He had to say something to her or do something with her. In the act of reciprocation there would at least be a third element, a merciful barrier between the polarities of their being.

But what could he say? He was incapable of being kind to her. To act was to be cruel – for in her presence he could only defend his guilt and to defend his guilt was to offend her. And to offend her was to make further communication impossible.

Suddenly, from far away, in a whimper of shock and resignation she said: 'I am afraid of you; you make me so afraid of you I dread even to speak.'

'Afraid of me?' he protested lamely. 'Oh, don't be mad.'

'I'm afraid it's so. There's nothing I can say to you. You hardly listen and when you do everything I say sounds stupid.'

'But that's just not true.'

'It is.'

There followed another long, unbearable interval of silence. But why did he not break it? he asked himself. Why did he not say something to her? Something kind. Something silly. Anything. Gradually, he began to face the fact that he found pleasure in the silence. His refusal to communicate was quite deliberate. It was he who had frozen himself into muteness. It was not that he would not say anything to her because he could not, but that he could not because he had chosen that he would not. It was his choice. And the choice was made simply and crudely for his own pleasure. His pleasure which rested in his awareness of her fear of him, her love, her bitterness, her silence.

But his consciousness, having freed itself in the stark confrontation of his choice, now left him open to his guilt. Slowly, it was catching up with him again. He sought a way out by being enraged with her. Suddenly he sprang up in the bed and cursed her.

'Why the hell don't you stop it?' he shouted. 'Stop playing the wounded martyr. Stop it! What do you want, anyway? Why do you torment me! Why the hell don't you leave me alone! What do you want? What do you want?'

But she only turned her head and stared at him and he could just see the gleam of her eyes where they were moist with anguish. He slumped back on the bed. There was no escape but to confront her. Suddenly he burst into tears.

'I never meant to hurt you... you must know I didn't. I tried... tried everything to keep us together... but it was no use; no use... all I ever succeeded in doing is hurting you. I... I don't know what to say... I...'

He buried his face in the pillow beside her and tried to compose himself. She moved closer to him and ran her hand over his back.

'You said yourself that you wanted no one else to have me,' she said. 'Why should you, if you did not care... even a little... there must have been something positive in your attraction for you not wanting so intensely anyone else to have me...'

'It was selfishness, I tell you, it sounds horrible, but that's the truth; I merely wished to possess you so that no one else could.'

'But even now you still feel this way; even now you still resent other men…'

'Yes, I know, I know; but that's no basis for any relationship. Oh Christ, can't you see how cruel I am to you? Do you think I enjoy it? Do you realise how much I despise myself when I consider how I've treated you?'

'Please tell me, then – and this is what I've been wanting to ask you all the time – why do you come back? Why do you keep coming back to me if your feelings are all so negative?'

He thought for a moment, for he himself was still uncertain of the nature of the force which had drawn him back to her. His thoughts still muffled, he tried to answer.

'I can't be sure. As I keep saying, it's partly guilt, partly the need for redemption. When I think of our relationship I can only see it for you as one long tragedy… Think of it… I got you pregnant when you were seventeen; you had to go off to New York to have the baby and then give it away, knowing how much you wanted to keep it… you know, I've not yet recovered from the shock of that experience yet… it messed up your studies, made you the subject of gossip for months… oh, when I think, when I think…'

'You don't have to remind me of all that, what I want to know is…'

'And there was the way I treated you after that… the other women, the quarrels, the insults… and even when I married you I did so knowing that I had not a drop of affection for you, doing it just to torture myself, to redeem my guilt…'

'Please,' she pleaded, 'there is no point recalling all that. It has happened. It is finished. What I want explained is just one thing: why do you come back, especially this last time? You went away to England to break it off completely. You claim to have fallen in love with some woman over there, then for some strange reason you suddenly packed up and left her and came back here to me; yet you still claim to love her. For God sake why do you do it? Is it that you enjoy torturing people? Or do you feel something for me which you are afraid to admit? I don't understand, I've given up trying. I want you to try and tell me why.'

'It's hard to explain. Especially with Elaine – well, how can you believe it. I love her, and that's why I left her, that's why I had to leave her. For to love someone implies some amount of belongingness, and this I was not prepared to accept. Crazy as it may sound, I loved her because she was the only woman who ever offered me the possibility of unattached involvement. She was always a thing apart. Separate. She was completely Anglo-Saxon, rooted in a past that was painstakingly obvious, totally involved in a culture that was every inch her own. I lacked not only the substance of such experiences, but even their form. It was not just that I was not Anglo-Saxon and had absolutely no desire to be one, but that the actual experience of being totally involved in a cultural complex such as hers was completely alien to me. Do you follow me?'

'I'm listening.' Her voice was timid with restraint. It was clear that to hear him speaking so dispassionately of his relation with another woman pained her. Yet she was deeply curious. He understood her feelings but was too used to hurting her to consider whether it would have been wise not to say anything more. In any event, it was at her request. So he continued, affecting an even greater air of detachment in the shallow hope that she would view the whole thing objectively.

'So it was then that I could love her as a person and yet not deny myself of the need for constant disengagement.'

'Are you saying that you loved her because she was Anglo-Saxon?'

'Good Lord, no! On the contrary, she was never an abstraction, there could be no one more flesh and blood than her. Oh I loved her as a person, as an individual being, all right. But it was the separateness of her culture and of her relation with it that made it possible for me to become involved with her. It mattered little that it was Anglo-Saxon; it could just as easily have been Japanese, or African or Indian. The important thing was that ultimately she could somehow be construed as separate, even if the everyday reality of our partial confrontation seemed constantly to have denied this. That way I could have my cake and eat it. With her I could be immediately involved yet ultimately unattached. And she made this easier for me by the quality of her own personality. For she remained a long time independent of me, despite her love. I hate to say this, but she did not love in the way you did. She never gave everything. She realised instinctively that it was unfair to love someone unselfishly in the way you did. To give everything is to demand everything. And the consciousness of the hopeless inability to fulfil even a fraction of that demand can only resolve itself in guilt. That's what happened to us. That's what killed our relationship.'

'So it's all my fault now,' she said.

'Oh no, no, no. I'm not blaming anybody. Perhaps you came to love me in the hopeless way you did because of my own treatment of you. It's too complicated. It's better to be simple-minded and say we just weren't meant for each other.'

'You still haven't explained why you left her and why you came back to me.'

'Well, it was partly Elaine, partly you. I felt I was losing out in my relationship with her. Don't ask me to explain what I mean by this. I'm not quite sure I know. We just reached a point where I could feel shades of dependence, and even worse, of commitment, creeping in. I'm not sure whether it was she who was becoming dependent on me, or me on her, or the both of us on each other. All I know is that there were moments when I could sense the same horrifying sense of commitment which I used to feel in relation to you. At the same time the safeguard of my cultural alienation from her was proving deceptive. I came to find out that the difference between someone who is completely rooted in a culture and another who has no roots in anything, as I am, has little to do with what they are or are not rooted in, but in the personal experience of their involvement. To a person who is totally involved, as she was, the whole problem of involvement is nonexistent. It's one hell of a paradox, but the problem of involvement or alienation, or whatever you want to call it, becomes real only in its absence. I found that out with her. Because of her assurance, because she took so much for granted what was the essence of all my concern, she could seek to bridge the gulf that separated us. And this I

couldn't take. It would have left me exposed, in sheer confrontation with her, as I was so often confronted with you. And you
know the consequences of that.'

'But why,' she asked, holding his arm gently, her voice confused but not lacking in sympathy, 'why are you so afraid of
confronting other people, as you put it. Why do you want to
remain isolated? Why do you complicate your life so much? Why
don't you just accept the fact of what you are?'

'And what the hell is that? You tell me.'

'A Jamaican for one…'

'Have you ever asked yourself what that is?'

'No, I never asked myself.'

'Exactly. The choice which this blasted place offers you is self-
imposed ignorance or the confrontation with barrenness. It's all
well and good when you spend your whole life here. Remain
smug, remain ignorant and remain insensitive and crude. This is
the creed of our soddy bourgeoisie. And my God you've got it bad!'

'I can't be blamed for never having had the opportunity of
breaking away,' she said bitterly.

'I'm sorry. I think you understand what I'm talking about. It's
those smug pack of bastards we go around with – George and
Edward and Neville and the whole goddamn lot of them. My
God, don't they for one moment ever pause to think, to reflect,
on what they are – what a cult of insensitivity?'

'And what are you?' she suddenly asked. The question took
him somewhat by surprise and he was sure he detected a note
either of sarcasm or malice in her voice. He looked down at her.
She seemed dazed and distant. He sighed.

'Nothing, I suppose. Just an absence of everything. I feel I want
to be something. The more important question is what I want to
be and to that I can only say that I want to be separate. I don't wish
to be involved or be committed to anything. I want to persist in
being unattached. Simply looking on. That way I can expect to be
everything. I can anticipate everything yet never experience the
shock of realising anything. I suppose in the end I'm just as
contemptible as all the rest of them. Basically I'm a coward, afraid
of all action, of all commitment. But I don't mind. I'm most at
ease with myself this way.'

'I don't understand you…' she began and then broke off halfheartedly.

'I'm sorry I can't make things any clearer. I'm confused myself. But believe me I never wished to hurt you. I know that in the end this is all I succeeded in doing. But it was my own dread of hurting you which partly resulted in it happening. When I was in England I kept thinking of you. As a matter of fact every time I thought of Jamaica I thought of you. You and this island became identified in the confused clouds of my imagination. You became lost in my nostalgia, in my desire to realise something here. It was only natural that when I came back here I should want to come back to you. For I share the same ambivalence to you that I share to the island: the grief, the aimlessness, the guilt and the commitment… well, not commitment, I should say, the desire for commitment. A desire which I couldn't help admitting was false, the result and the cause of my guilt. Oh how did I ever get in such an emotional mess, how, how? You had the misfortune to be mixed up in it all. And see what happened…'

His voice trailed off to a whisper. He stopped speaking and gazed at the ceiling. They remained mute, unthinking. Suddenly, he seemed to respond to something in the silence. His mind seemed made up as he rose from the bed and began to put on his clothes. She suddenly became aware of his actions and realised, at last, that it was the end.

In panic, she sprang from the bed and held on to him. 'No, no; don't leave me,' she cried, 'not just yet, not now, please.'

'I'm going.'

She fell at his feet, held on to his legs and wept.

'What happened to you?' she asked between her tears. 'What have you become? Why are you doing this to yourself?'

He felt silly. He thought there was something absurdly melo-dramatic about her, about their situation. He became annoyed, impatient, and pushed her away, saying he was sorry. She re-mained where she fell on the floor, weeping.

He dressed hurriedly and was soon ready.

'I'll send someone round to collect my things,' he said.

He was devoid of all emotions. He stared at her blankly, feeling no longer anything of guilt, or shame or remorse. At last she was just something, another person. Apart. He felt a bit bored and tired, but slightly relieved.

'See you around,' he said, and left.

# 3

'Oh, so you did decide to grace us with your presence,' Edward said as he opened the door for Alexander. He had a wide, rueful grin which made it impossible to decide whether his sarcasm was genuine or not.

'Come in,' he added with a toss of his head towards the small group inside. There were six of them, including Edward, and they sat in a semicircle around an occasional table on which was a bottle of rum, a jug of water, some ice and a copy of the latest issue of the government's five-year plan.

Lloyd, a stocky, dark lecturer with malicious, intelligent black eyes, was in the process of tearing the contents of the plan to pieces when Alexander entered. He paused for a brief moment to grunt a folksy 'Wha' 'appen, ol' man,' then continued with his tirade. 'They've sold us out,' he was saying. 'They've sold out the only goddamn piece of wealth in the country. They sold us out.' He kept pointing aggressively at the green-covered book on the table and, in his usual manner, repeated himself over and over with ever-increasing animation.

Lloyd was a rabid socialist and occupied the role of official theoretician for the group. He had a sharp incisive mind, but his method of arguing seemed always to conspire to hide the fact. He seemed to be deathly serious, yet his earnestness was tempered so heavily with a strange, mocking self-irony that it was difficult to take him entirely seriously. The rest of the group, who knew him well and were greatly influenced by him, were a perfect foil for his peculiar type of critical self-parodying animosity. At everything he said they shook their heads, cursed, laughed a little, then ended their response on a note of seriousness by cursing again.

'What's eating you now?' Alex asked.

'What's eating us? What's eating us? Just take a look at that agreement which the government reached with the bauxite companies over royalties. Or just glance at the whole plan. No imagination. No imagination at all. A few more jobs for the boys. A few more housing estates for the civil servants. A few more palliatives for the slum districts and that's all. That's all. It's a disgrace; it's a scandal.'

'But what else did you expect?'

'Now listen,' Edward exclaimed, 'if you're going to start with this cynical bull-shit you can leave my house right now!' He walked towards the door and began to open it, grinning sheepishly.

'Hold it, fellows; hold it, fellows,' Lloyd said, raising his hand and bowing his head in a gesture of moderation. 'Let us be calm and rational about this thing. If we're to get anywhere we must be calm and rational; we must organise; you hear me, we must organise. There's no room for in-group fighting.'

Alex had got up to go and Lloyd came across to him, forcing him back down on his chair. 'Have another drink,' he said, pouring him a heavy Appleton.

'I won't be insulted,' Alex said as he sat down, not intending the statement to mean anything. He took a heavy swig at the rum and made a luscious grimace as he wiped his mouth with the back of his hand.

Suddenly he became aware of the unusual silence in the room and began to look awkwardly around at everyone. They were all staring at him, a mild tint of humour on their faces. He almost blushed as he said, 'Hello, hello; what's up; have you all lost your tongues suddenly; has my presence deprived you of speech; or are you waiting for me to say something?' He paused, but they remained silent. Carmen, sitting in an armchair, with her legs crossed, in one corner, lit a cigarette. He glanced at her and had a mild shock.

The woman was attractive. No, but she was. He had seen her about since he returned from England but had never taken any particular interest in her. If anything, he had thought her rather sloppy, especially the way her short hair with the faded tint stuck up on her head like a senseh-fowl. Now the impact she had on

61

him was entirely different. It wasn't just that her hair had recently been combed, and brushed smooth on her head, brought out all the lengthy, slanted elegance of her face. Perhaps it was the way she crossed her legs so that her tight jersey frock crept halfway up her thighs. Her long, brown legs, sculptured together, had a startling, serpentine fullness about them. His eyes crept up to the rest of her body. Yes, she was even beautiful. The fact that he hadn't realised it all along only heightened the present impact. From across the room he could sense, almost feel, the rhythm of her body. And there was her posture. The natural elegance. The careless grace which dared vulgarity to the point of revealing her black underwear, yet transcending it with a wry, lethargic beauty.

Lloyd finally broke the silence. He cleared his throat and, in an air of extreme gravity, addressed Alex.

'We'll get to the point, Alex, and start by telling you why we asked you over this afternoon.'

'Good.'

'Ever since we had our little disagreement…'

'Disagreement…?' Alex queried.

'Well, you know. . .'

Lloyd, for the first time since Alex knew him, seemed almost embarrassed. He was delighted and so added ruthlessly, 'Oh, you mean since I was purged from the group.'

'Nobody purged you; we just didn't see eye to eye on certain issues and gave you an ultimatum.'

'Oh, cut out all this bull-shit,' Edward put in brashly. 'Let's keep to the point.'

'Take it easy,' Lloyd repeated. 'Take it easy. Well, anyway, Alex, the men have been reconsidering and decided we should give you another chance to explain your situation.'

Edward gave a mocking grunt as he drank his rum, which left no doubt about his part in the decision Lloyd spoke of. Lloyd gave him another cautious glance and continued:

'We want to know where you stand, man; I mean, we just can't accept the fact that you've opted out on the movement. It just doesn't seem possible. We want to know where you stand.'

'Where I stand?'

'Yes; your position. How you see the situation.'

'But I told you a million times already, Lloyd; I have no position; and for God's sake don't tell me that that itself is a position or I'll scream.'

Lloyd gave a quick glance around the room as if to muster support. None was forthcoming, so he took another sip of rum, lit a cigarette and continued with renewed gusto.

'Well, look; let's begin with fundamentals; let's start where everything must start – the people; the workers. Now, you know the situation, Alex. You can't help knowing the situation: you live in it; at one time you even studied it. We have a country – not a poor country, mind you; perhaps not a rich one, but one with adequate resources – and what we find in this country. Poverty. Vicious abstract poverty. Twenty per cent unemployment. Slums. Degradation. Demoralisation. Now tell me, Alex, how can you live in a situation like this and you don't take a position? Man, you must either be a bourgeois or a capitalist committed to the *status quo;* or you must be against it…'

And her eyes were wide and slanted and a dark, churney brown. She kept inhaling and blowing out the fumes of her cigarette in that careless manner of hers. Yet she did not give the impression of boredom or even indifference. As he glanced over at her he could see she was totally aware of everything that was being said. At the same time the expression would seem to suggest that what she was aware of was absolutely unimportant. She was there; sitting down with crossed legs; facing him. But she was more than there. Her presence filled the room; was too much for the room. She was really too much there. So he could not be sure that despite the ever-growing impact of her presence he had grasped it in its entirety. Why had he not felt the same about her all along. How could he have missed her. Man, was he living?

'You listening, Alex?'

'I'm hearing you.'

'Well then, tell us.'

'Tell you what?'

'Tell us how… how in the name of God you can remain uncommitted in a situation like this.'

'What is there to be committed to?' His voice was distant. She had large, beautifully moulded breasts. Two graceful domes; vibrant; compelling.

'The people, man; the people. In a situation like this it's criminal to remain indifferent.'

'As a matter of fact, Alex,' Joyce put in, 'it's more moral to be against them than to be indifferent to them. At least then, after the revolution, we can shoot you with an absolutely clear conscience.'

There was a roar of laughter.

'I don't know what you're talking about, Joyce,' Edward added icily. 'I could always shoot this bastard with a clear conscience.'

She only smiled a little. A lazy, nonchalant smile. Things were clearly too unimportant for her to be malicious.

'But what about them?' Alex said.

'Them? Who?' Lloyd asked.

'The people you speak of.'

'What about them? I've told you.'

'Yes, but you didn't say how they felt about the matter.'

'How they felt about the matter? Can there be any doubt about that?'

'Perhaps not; the way you see it. But listen, Lloyd, I've told you already. I don't think, I don't feel I have any right to be responsible for other people. It's difficult enough being responsible for myself to take on the responsibility of a whole mass of people. As far as I am concerned that's gross pretentiousness. If you all want to it's all right by me; and the best of luck. But I can't; I don't feel I have the right.'

'Oh, Alex, Alex, Alex, my brother,' Lloyd said with heart-grinding concern, 'what do you want? What really do you want?'

'Nothing that I know of.'

'But you must, man. It's not possible that you don't. Certainly not in the position you're in. I'm telling you, man, you're committed, whether you like it or not. Let me spell it out for you since some crazy cloud has blinded you temporarily. You're a black man; a Negro. And you live in a white world. Perhaps not in Jamaica, but this land is firmly in the West. Uncle Sam's breathing down our backside every moment. Literally. Make Edward tell you about the two C.I.A. agents he caught tailing him after he came back from Cuba. And it's not just America. The colonial past is still here in this country. It was your very social analysis which proved this without a doubt. We are black men in a white civilisation and whether you like it or not you're committed to the freedom of your race…'

The glow of her rich cinnamon skin was almost tangible. She remained perfectly still, yet there was an intense rhythm in the symmetry of her body. Carmen. The name fitted her. Carmen. Carmen. Carmen…

'…and that is not all. There is your country. This land. Our land which we must save from the neo-imperialists. This people. Our people, which we must save from poverty. Which we must mobilise into action. And there is yourself which you must save from the corrupt bourgeois background we live in. Man, how can you sit there and tell me that you are not committed, that you don't want to do anything?'

'That was a great speech, Lloyd, but I'm afraid it left me cold. I've told you before, if I don't know what I want I at least know what I don't want. I don't want to be categorised. I don't want to be labelled and compartmentalised into little pigeonholes of abstractions, no matter how large, no matter how important they may seem. I don't want to spend my life *being* a Negro or being a Jamaican or being a socialist or a capitalist or what you like. I'm goddamn sick and tired of the whole damn' process. I'm bored, absolutely bored with being things, with being abstractions. If you must know, I simply want to be me, to be what I am. And that alone takes a lifetime of knowing. And until I know that any attempt at being Jamaican or socialist or reactionary or Negro or what you like is just jumping the gun. As far as I'm concerned all I'd be then would be simply a model of paper labels which tears easily and is all hollow inside. I'm sorry, man; there's not much point us arguing about the subject. Sometime in the future perhaps…'

'There will be no future for you, man,' Edward put in acidly.

'How wonderful to hear,' Alex retorted, getting up to pour himself another drink. He clinked the glass on Edward's and added, 'Now perhaps we can drink and be friends again.'

'Reactionary bastard,' Edward toasted, and they both drank together.

Politics over, Alex pulled Edward to one corner and in a hushed voice enquired, 'Do you know her well?'

'I saw you staring at her; was that why you were talking so much crap?'

'But seriously; what do you know about her?'

'We spend the occasional weekend together.'

'So she's swinging, eh?'

'You can put it that way; but I wouldn't try if I were you.'

'Why not?'

'For one, I'm still keen on her; and in any case you can't handle that beast.'

'We'll see about that,' Alex said, this time loudly, thumping Edward in the groin jokingly.

They had both known each other from secondary school and had remained friends largely because of their willingness to be ruthless and hostile to each other. At school and at university they had exchanged places at the top of their classes. With the exception of cricket, which offered little scope for violence, they had shared an equal dislike for games, and a prodigiously early passion for women. In the latter they were totally unscrupulous with each other, even to the point of Edward making not a few attempts at seducing Pauline. Edward, more than any other person, appreciated the complexities of the relationship between Alex and Pauline. He fully understood the guilt, the soul-consuming claustrophobia which Alex experienced with her, and, for this very reason, had been most strenuous in his efforts at keeping them together. At the same time no one castigated the insinuation of marriage as much as he did. What complicated the situation even more was that they both liked and attracted the same women.

Yet their very lack of loyalty to each other held between them the only real respect they held for anyone. For Edward, despite his socialist commitments, despite his political demagoguery, was at heart a complete cynic. What they both liked about each other was the complete freedom, the complete lack of any commitment or responsibility in their relationship. There was no loyalty and so there could be no demands. They could hate and despise each other when it suited them to hate and despise each other. And when friendship was necessary it could be arranged. Because they were so absolutely contemptible with each other they could be absolutely human. Deep down they always felt something a little refreshing in the complete honesty of their frequent encounters.

Alex walked slowly across to the corner where Carmen was sitting. Seeing her glass empty, he asked her if he could pour her another drink. She smiled, a little wryly, and extended her hand with the glass.

'Just a little ice with it please,' she said. As he walked across to the table he could sense that she was staring at him. She still was when he returned. There was nothing brash or challenging or suspicious in her stare. Nor was it an attempt at being coy. She simply looked at him out of a blank, not very encouraging, curiosity.

'Thanks,' she said, as she took the glass of rum and he sat down beside her. Then she looked away and her eyes fell vacantly on the yellowish-brown contents of the glass before her. Slowly, she began to shake the glass; producing a nagging, irregular sound with the tinkling of the ice.

Alex, for perhaps the first time in the presence of a woman, began to feel awkward. What was he to do or say? She had none of the conventional postures of her sex. There was neither coyness, nor brashness, nor niceness, nor any of the forced just-an-ordinary-girlness he had grown accustomed to find in Jamaican women. She simply sat there before him, lazily casual, disconcertingly relaxed. Finally he ventured very uncertainly:

'I can't imagine how we never met before.'

'I've seen you around,' she replied; 'you were just too busy with your domestic problems I guess.'

'That Edward!' he said with an affectation of anger. She smiled and said facetiously, 'We all have our little problems, I guess.'

'Yes; and they are all such bores.'

'Do you think so? I would have thought the opposite was true. Our little problems come to rescue us from our boredom so often. I don't know what I'd do without the occasional problem of finding an abortionist; or a dead relative; or even being heavily in debt.'

He wasn't sure about the tone of her voice. He had the

impression that there was a certain ring of contempt for every-thing she herself said. Speaking, it would seem, was hardly worth the effort. Yet she did not seem particularly averse to his presence. If contact could only begin with the convention of speech, well then, they might as well speak on.

'Yet,' she continued distantly, 'I guess even the problems that offer a refuge from boredom themselves become a bore after a time.'

'I bet they can,' Alex said, at last beginning to adjust to her mood. 'Getting an abortion in this island can be a dreary affair.'

'Your ideas don't seem to be very popular among your friends, at least not these here,' she said, changing the subject. Her eyes had suddenly lit up and for one brief moment she seemed genuinely involved in what she was saying. And the apparent involvement, if ever so slight and transient, came as a pleasant surprise in contrast to her usual nonchalance. This fascinated him. He began to feel that hidden below the outward show of vacancy there was something strange, exciting and beautiful, which only occasionally erupted to the surface of her being in the brief, stark, little snatches of interest she had a way of suddenly exhibiting in what surrounded her.

Instead of answering her Alex asked:

'How come you are mixed up with this group of inquisitors, anyway?'

'Oh, I just happened to have spent the night with Edward and was too lazy to go away, especially since Joyce was here. Besides, one might just as well be an active revolutionary as be an inactive conservative.'

'What do you do when you aren't being bored by would-be politicians?'

'Nothing, really.'

'Nothing?'

'I suppose that's all one can call it; although at times I'm not sure I succeed even in that.'

'And have you always done only nothing?'

'No; I was in the Civil Service.'

'Well; I can always understand anyone quitting that.'

'I didn't; they fired me.'

'Fired you! From the Service?'

'Yes,' she said, and giggled idly.

'That must be a record; whatever for?'

'Oh, I just didn't turn up for work too often... didn't feel like it. One morning the head of the department called me and began to raise hell, asking for an explanation. I told him I had screwed with three men the night before and was too exhausted to come to work in the morning, or to do anything, for that matter. He asked me to leave. So I left.'

'Yes; I can imagine you were tired,' Alex commented, making his voice as neutral as he possibly could.

'We are having a thing around our place tonight; would you like to come?'

'Love to.'

'It's at Joyce's really; I'm bumming along at her place at the moment. You'll come, won't you?' she said, getting up and stretching.

Again there was the surprise of real interest coming when it was least expected. A second earlier he had meant, in fact, not to go. In his state of mind, he felt the last person he could want to spend an evening with was someone as indifferent as she was. But in the very act of stretching, her 'You'll come, won't you?' suggested a degree of interest and desire which, crass as he felt his response was, rather flattered him. Her supreme nonchalance, with its little hints of self-destruction nibbling at him, seemed to present a challenge. Was it possible that he had completely misinterpreted her? Perhaps, after all, she was just a crashing bore who knew no better than to fart her time away. Perhaps she was just a perfectly normal woman playing an unusually ingenious act. Or perhaps she was what he first thought – a profoundly sensitive person, too much involved with the sheer trauma of facing herself to be involved with anything else. Whatever, it would be worth finding out.

The party itself was something of a bore. The same loud, popular music, mainly ska; the same semi-professional, semi-academic crowd aggressively identifying with the masses in the same self-consciously vulgar manner; the same couple of English lecturers next-door phoning and complaining with the same irate response: 'But what a nerve! If this isn't our own country...' the same trite talk over glasses of rum and ginger: 'Isn't the Governor-General a silly fool? Did you hear what his wife did when Princess Mary visited King's House.' 'Yes; but you must admit, he's a man of the people...'

Alex sat outside on the lawn with a flask of rum, staring vacantly at the street-light. When he arrived he had spotted Carmen dancing energetically with a youth who could be no more than seventeen. The youth was agile and nimble on his feet and a small group stood around shouting admiringly at them. When she saw him she ran from the dance floor to meet him on the veranda, hugged him to her tightly, and before he had breath to say hello had kissed him passionately on his mouth.

'Great of you to come,' she said, the sweat running down her neck, on to her breasts. She seemed in great spirits, and an intoxicating aroma of rum, sweat and perfume poured from her. As suddenly as she had greeted him she abandoned him, saying in a loud whisper that she would see him later. Then she went back to the youth, who had remained on the dance floor staring, baffled, at them. He seemed a little hurt when she returned, but she settled that by kissing him gently on his ear, ruffling his hair and laughing teasingly at him. Not long after she had lured him into one of the bedrooms and was still there when, an hour or so later, Alex decided he had had enough of dancing and had gone and sat on the veranda.

But there was little peace to be had. Edward had come and teased him, saying he couldn't imagine what it felt like to be humiliated.

'I don't know what the hell you're talking about,' Alex replied. 'You're the one who should be humiliated; she's your woman, isn't she?'

'My woman; I never said anything of the sort; Carmen is nobody's woman; you make the most of her when she's willing, and when she leaves you thank God for small mercies. But you, you, my friend; I could see how your mind ran today. I could see you with your infantile, immature little mind concocting dreams of taming her. Damn bourgeois bastard; all you know to do is to tame and domesticate and exploit. Ha! Did you think she had fallen head over heels for you? Would you be the man, the great lover, that would give her what no one else had given her? Would you…?'

'Come off it, will you; the place is noisy enough as it is; you do like to talk a lot of shit sometimes.'

'You know it's true; that's why you're losing your temper.'

'Losing my temper? Listen, what's eating you?'

He laughed loud and jeeringly. It was his most likeable feature, this rich, uninhibited laughter of his. In his nastiest moments he would suddenly hold his head high and burst into it, and no matter how mocking the emotion that had stimulated his mirth there was always the feeling that such a pure, spontaneous laughter must somehow have an element of kindness in it. Alex smiled a little, putting his glass to his lips so as not to be detected, then turned his back on Edward, who had already begun to walk away.

Not long after another plague appeared in the guise of John Fitzmaurice, a Jamaican physicist at the university. Alex held an open dislike and contempt for him, but somehow had never managed to avoid meeting him at almost every party he went, especially since Fitzmaurice seemed to have a great fondness for talking to him. What Alex could not stand most about him was his utter phoneyness. Fitzmaurice was what one could glibly dismiss as a black Englishman. His manners, his speech, his gestures, even, at times, his dress, appeared completely English. This in itself was, to Alex, not so much irritating as sad and pathetic. But on closer acquaintance Fitzmaurice turned out to be a far more complex and certainly less sympathetic person than the usual black Englishman, an element of which, after all, was inevitably to be found in any Jamaican. What was most distasteful about him was the utter bad faith with which he handled his Englishness. Being acutely conscious of it, and of its absurdity in the eyes of everyone he confronted, he constantly sought to parody himself. Thus his Oxford accent was just that little bit overdone in such a way that it became obvious to everyone that he was consciously over-doing it. So it was with his gestures, and his movements, which he over-affected to the point of femininity. The result of

71

this self-caricature was laughter and general amusement among his acquaintances, an amusement which he himself never failed to share. In this way he had acquired some sort of a reputation as a wit. It was a subtle and, to Alex, contemptible technique, for his whole personality embodied, and went so much to the heart of, what was most distasteful about bourgeois Jamaicans. Few people could have had their cake and ate it as ferociously as Fitzmaurice. Not only was his desire to be English somewhat tenuously satisfied, but the insecurities and self-contempt which it implied were allayed, indeed smothered, both in himself and those around him by caricaturing and laughing at it.

At that moment Alex was in no mood for indulging anyone, least of all Fitzmaurice, and he felt that the only alternative to leaving the party was to be rude.

'You're still at it, I see,' Alex greeted him coldly.

'And what may that be, dear boy?' was Fitzmaurice's sweet retort.

'Being goddamn phoney.'

'I say, you are rather peeved tonight, aren't you, old boy? Perhaps we'd better talk about it.' He pulled up a chair, sat down, crossed his legs slowly and elegantly with a gleam of humorous expectancy in his eyes. Alex stared at him vilely.

'You know, Fitzmaurice, you are amazing...'

'Well, between the two of us, old boy, I always suspected that myself,' he butted in, and laughed boisterously, looking around to make sure that his reputation as a wit was making its impression. Without the slightest change of expression Alex continued:

'You are the only person I know who pretends to be not what you are by pretending to be what you are.'

Fitzmaurice, finally sensing Alex's coldness, now stared at him with a look of utter perplexity.

'Come again, old chap,' he said feebly.

'You heard me the first time,' Alex replied flatly.

'Yes, but I'm not quite sure I understand you.'

'Don't you?'

There was a period of silence in which Alex outstared the other man. The latter eventually looked away, flushed, and, suddenly collecting himself, jumped up from his chair, placed his arms akimbo in the manner of the peasants and in flat dialect bellowed: 'Is wha' 'appen to dis man; who' me do you, sah?' This sudden resort to the vernacular, characteristic of him, struck Alex as perhaps the most obnoxious feature of Fitzmaurice's phoneyness. It was his clumsy, hopelessly naive, way of responding to anyone who saw through his pathetic pretences. In fact it was merely a reverse form of the phoneyness which was his normal person. For he used the dialect in the same grotesquely affected manner that he used his Oxford accent – averting contempt by the same technique of anticipating it in his all too obvious self-mockery. Alex continued to stare at him coldly. In even more embarrassment Fitzmaurice shouted for everyone to hear:

'Me rass-cloth; see here! Something wrong with dis chappy, you know; 'im not all here. I don't trouble de man an' 'im just start to pick on me. But lawd me God.'

Several people on the veranda looked around and laughed. Alex only noted that a further dimension was added to Fitzmaurice's hypocrisy by virtue of the fact that his last outburst was expressed not so much in an affected dialect but more in the manner of someone affecting an Englishman affecting the dialect. This coincidence of acute hypocrisy Alex felt to be the very limit. He shook his head slowly and said under his breath, loud enough for Fitzmaurice to hear: 'You are contemptible.'

Fitzmaurice, after once more taking hold of himself, smothered all by suddenly bursting out laughing – as if to give the impression that Alex's last remark had been a private joke between them – and while rather boldly patting him on the shoulder, remarked loudly and indulgently:

'My friends; my friends.' Then he fled to the back veranda.

Not long after, Joyce, who was giving the party, came over and said hello. She was a woman for whom Alex had a rather negative admiration. Tall, massive and coal black, she was a kind of modern intellectual version of the classical Negro matriarch. What should have been a severe inferiority complex over both her colour and her size was sublimated by an acute intelligence into a lively, boisterously domineering personality. She spoke in a loud, raw-chaw manner, her posture always one of utter relaxation, which was all the more remarkable considering her size, caring little for what people said and thought of her. This was just as well. Most decent Jamaican ladies detested her, claiming her to be vulgar, immoral and loud, which indeed she was. Partly for these reasons, and for her sophisticated rationalisation of herself and what she stood for, she had acquired a certain vogue among the more progressive men at the university. But she could be ruthless, both in the Rabelaisian ferocity with which she bullied her men into bed, and, no less often, out of it.

'What tricks you up to now?' he asked her, laughing lazily. She laughed in her deliciously vulgar fashion and, after lighting a cigarette and sticking it at the corner of her large, beautifully sculpted lips, placed her head confidingly close to his and whispered in a hoarse voice:

'Alex; there is a man inside there which I swear to God I going to lay tonight.'

'Who's that?'

'Mind your own business.'

'Come on, come on; what's the use of being malicious without knowing who you're being malicious about?'

She took a deep drag on the cigarette, and turned her head round to look at someone dancing inside. Alex looked in her direction and saw the professor of international law.

'Not him!'

She replied with a mischievous giggle.

'Oh, have a heart, Joyce. The man is happily married. His wife is a good girl. She'd die if she heard about it.'

'Good girl? Is what wrong with you? She's the biggest bitch on campus.'

'Why do you think so?'

'She is a real bourgeois fart; go about the place spreading all sort of gossip about other women's husbands. You know what she went and told Carl's wife the other day?'

'You mean about him and the Chinese student?'

'Yes; and it's not Carl alone; women like that must be put in their place. You don't know nothing, you know. None of you men know anything. It's not the men who bugger up this society; it's the women!'

Having, inevitably, worked her way around to her favourite

topic – the pernicious influence of women on Jamaican society – Alex realised that there was little he could do but listen, since he was in no mood to out-shout her. Besides, he rather agreed with most of what she had to say, and it was always a gratifying experience hearing it coming from a woman. She pulled up her chair closer to him, crossed her legs the other way, then began to puff on her cigarette aggressively, as was her manner whenever she ventured on to one of her pet subjects.

'Now you listen to me, Alex; I'm speaking from the inside, so I know what I talking about. These bitches have to be changed completely before anything can be done about this country. You hear me? I don't know how you going to do it; all I know is that before any substantial change take place in this here island you've got to get hold of every one of these bitches and turn them inside out. Every one of them: upper class, middle class and lower class. They dominate the men when they growing up. They turn all you men into a pack of raving neurotics. They make you twisted, ambivalent and irresponsible. You hear lots of talk about those lazy kiss-me-ass bastards who refuse to work; there is only one way to change them and that is to change the kind of mothers that produce them.'

'Aren't you putting the cart before the horse,' Alex butted in, rather lamely, knowing full well the response.

'That's a load of shit, man. Don't give me any of that crap about men's double standards. It's not men who make women what they are. It's the other way around. At least it's been so in this island ever since the first slave realised that to every one woman about the place there were three of him. It's the woman who has messed up this island; I tell you more, it's the woman who has messed up the Negro race; and I couldn't care a damn about first causes. What I'm interested in is now. Now! As of this moment! If you want change you've got to change them. And while you and Lloyd and Edward quarrel about ideological crap, me and one or two others are tackling the real problem. And we doing it the best way we know how. By fighting them with their own weapon. Using the tools that God give us. You've got to begin by jolting those bitches. You've got to shock them and hurt them. And the best way to do it is to hit them where it hurt most – their men. You follow me?'

'I'm struggling along.'

'How do you think, for example, the professor's wife will react when she find out that I seduce her husband? Is trauma, you know. Is shame and shock and dismay she going to feel when she realise that me, a woman like me, got her husband where I want him. And after that she'll never be the same person again. Take my word. And as a Jamaican woman talking to a Jamaican man, I have the right to dominate you. You listen to me. Before any political or social or what-not revolution take place in this country there is one revolution which have to take place. A unique revolution. You hear me, boy! A unique revolution. For the weapon you have to use is sex. And the battleground will be the bed!'

She suddenly sprang up, spat her cigarette from her lips and laughed rebelliously.

'I have a mission to perform,' she whispered wickedly. Then she made for the professor.

After she left he took up his chair and went out on the lawn. It was while he was sitting there staring at the street-light about an hour later that someone crept up softly behind him and ran her fingers across his neck. He looked up and saw Carmen.

She smiled sheepishly down at him, giggled a little, then sat down on the arm of his chair.

'You aren't angry with me, are you?'

'Now why should I be?' he said calmly.

'Edward seem to have thought so,' she laughed.

He returned her smile and continued to stare at the lamppost. He could tell from the fresh odour of her skin that she had just showered. He wondered idly what she would look like naked under a shower, at the same time turning and looking at her. His eyes rested on the mould of her breasts. She had nothing underneath her loose cotton dress, for he could just detect the form of her nipples under the cloth. He stretched his neck out and held the cloth around her nipples gently between his teeth. She winced suddenly with laughter and fell upon his thighs. As she laughed she gave her body up to the night. Her limbs fell freely about him and he had to make an effort to prevent her from falling.

Then she was quiet and her large, slanted brown eyes stared blankly at the vast emptiness of the greyish-blue sky.

'There are no stars up there tonight,' she said in a distant voice.

'I guess not,' he answered without looking up.

'I prefer it like that,' she added, remotely, idly.

'Do you? Why?'

'Why? Why? How should I know why? Because stars are so gaudy, I suppose. But then, why should I hate them because they are gaudy? I have nothing against gaudiness. Do you have anything against gaudiness?'

'I don't know; it depends on the circumstances.'

'Depends on the circumstances...' she repeated, her voice trailing off. What she said was said in such a manner that it was utterly pointless. She played with speech. She mocked it. Nothing, it seemed, was worth saying, and it was wonderful how she said it. Her voice was like her limbs – its lazy tremor, the frequency with which it was stifled up in her throat, its facetious, low-pitched monotony, gave the impression always that it was somehow on its own, quite reluctantly making the effort of having itself heard.

'Depends on the circumstances,' she repeated. 'Most well spoken, my clever scholar. Depends on the circumstances. Everything depends on the circumstances; and I suppose everything depends equally not on the circumstances. Am I not clever? If after you make love to me tonight, assuming that you are interested, you give me a pound for services rendered, then I'm a whore. But what happens if the circumstances are different...'

Again the idle pause. Her left hand dangled freely from one side of the chair, with her fingertips touching the ground. She flicked up a blade of grass and began to chew it.

'...Where were we, my scholar?... Yes... the circumstances are different. Tomorrow morning you shall buy me a present. Perhaps you shall give me a copy of your latest book... that costs roughly a pound. I am no longer a whore. Then I'm simply a with-it female intellectual. Isn't it remarkable?... Isn't it absolutely remarkable, my dear scholar, how thin the difference is between a simple whore and a complex female intellectual... but wait, wait,' her voice acquired a mocking sense of urgency, 'let us pare the edges even thinner – supposing my dear scholar… supposing that instead of buying your book for me you gave me a pound instead and said that I should buy it, then my being a whore will have boiled down simply to whether I bought your book or not… so, you see, despite how much you may deride it, your book on Race does have some value, after all… just think, dear scholar, the reputation of a dark maiden such as me… I… may well depend entirely on it… how remarkable… how absolutely remarkable…'

'A most ingenious deduction, my dear Carmen,' he said, imitating her tone.

Suddenly she sprang up. 'Let us dance,' she said.

'Out here?'

'Yes; why not? I like to dance on the lawn.'

So they danced. She held him closely and, without moving her feet, swayed to the rhythm of the calypso. She kissed him once more on his lips, then on his neck. Then she held back her head and laughed a little at the sky. After the long silence that followed she said:

'You do despise me, don't you?'

'Good Lord; despise you? Whatever for?'

'You know you do. You are the type who despises everything…'

'That's not a nice thing to say.'

'Oh, not that I blame you for it. As a matter of fact, it's something to be admired. Despite what you say, you still feel strongly about things; you can still pass judgement on things; even if it's all only negative. But that at least is something.'

He looked down at her but said nothing. She sighed deeply and he felt a sudden tinge of warmth for her.

'I wish I could at least condemn things. Say they are wrong, all wrong, if even I don't know how to set them right.'

'I can't say I'm as positive as you make me out to be. I certainly don't feel strongly about much. It's more a matter of opting out…'

'Yes, but at least you've made up your mind what you don't want. You've declared yourself against everything, which is the beginning of preparing yourself for everything. No?'

'You're more sensible than I thought.'

'Aha. Well, my reputation is saved, then. Tomorrow morning you shall present me with a complimentary copy of your book.'

He laughed. She laughed. Between them came the monotonous beat of the music; the prattle of the crowd inside.

'The dew is falling,' she said.

'Do you want to go inside?'

'Not just yet. I don't mind the dew. I'm in love with the dew, did I not tell you?'

'No. Why do you love the dew?'

'Oh, I love anything which creeps up in the night and flees in the morning. Day is too serious for it. What am I saying? Am I not silly?'

Suddenly her life seemed to have vanished. Her whole body slumped about him and he held on to her just in time to prevent them both falling.

'Are you all right?'

She did not answer. He struggled towards the chair and she fell over him, her head dangling over the arm of the chair.

'You must despise me,' she said in a remote, careless tone. 'It must be wonderful to be able to despise everybody; everything...'

'Crazy woman.'

'Not crazy... nothing as complex as that... just an aimless drifter. Possessing not even the effort to despise anything, not even myself. A feather for every wind that blows...'

Then she made a childlike imitation of the wind blowing, moving her hand awkwardly to the sound.

'I'm tired,' she said eventually. 'Come to bed with me and keep me company. We can have fun in the morning.'

## 4

They were beautiful days. They were careless days. Irresponsible days. Days of idleness. Days without thought. Days devoid of anticipation, contemptuous of the future. Days without memory, oblivious of the past. Each moment was taken for what it was, accepted on its own terms, rejected on its own terms.

We tasted everything that was in the offing – passion, laughter, poetry, picnics by the sea, walks in the mountains – we chewed upon them. What we cared for we swallowed. What we didn't like we spat out. But, really, it mattered little whether we swallowed or rejected, for they were all the same, simply a moment of experience. And there was as much idleness, as much reality, in the swallowing as in the spitting.

For nothing possessed meaning beyond itself, beyond the moment of our confrontation with it. Intrinsically everything was beautifully meaningless; so extrinsically everything could have as much meaning as it cared to offer, as we cared to accept.

We sought only to exploit each other. In bed we were selfish, ruthless, seeking only to exhaust the other until we both ended exhausted. Day and night lost their meaning, their rhythm. For we woke when we were bored with sleeping; and we slept when we were bored with waking.

In conversation – if what we said to each other could be called conversation, for meaning had somehow come to lose all content, something absurd, to be played at, laughed at, laughed with – we were merciless with each other. There was no sparing of feelings; no sense of protection. Each of us was there as the foil of the other's humour, of the other's mockery, of the other's sadness.

There were times when we played with the notion of love.

'Tell me that you love me,' she would say. 'Tell me how

virginal I am, how innocent I look, in your own eyes. Come on, let us play being sentimental.'

Then I would whisper sweet things to her and she would laugh, almost hysterically. Eventually she would ask me to read a piece of poetry for her. Always it was the same verse from the same poem: the second stanza of Donne's 'A Nocturnall Upon St. Lucies Day'. I would read the lines with an affectation of passion and sincerity:

> *Study me then, you who shall lovers bee*
> *At the next world, that is, at the next Spring:*
> *For I am every dead thing,*
> *In whom love wrought new Alchemie.*
> *For his art did expresse*
> *A quintessence even from nothingnesse,*
> *From fell privations, and leane emptinesse*
> *He ruin'd mee, and I am re-begot*
> *Of absence, darknesse, death; things which are not.*

And her response was always the same. When I finished reading she would fall into an enigmatic silence. Her eyes became wistful and sad and she seemed on the point of tears. At first I laughed, thinking how cleverly she plays her part. But her persistence begins to cast me in doubt. Could she be serious? Had she played herself into reality? Or, worse, was it a covert reality which had induced her, in the first place, to play itself?

'Say, what's going on?' I begin anxiously. Then she would stare blandly at me and there would be a long maddening moment in which I was crippled with indecision as to whether she was a perfect actress or a perfect maniac. Finally, just at the point where I was about to hold her and shake her, she would burst out laughing, pointing her finger and turning the whole joke on me, saying wildly that she was sure I would have loved her to be as she was acting. And there was little I could do but join her mocking laughter.

There was no possession, for we both claimed absolutely, and gave nothing. So we continued in a delirious stalemate.

And we kept clear, wonderfully clear, of any real involvement with each other. The sweet languor of the mornings. The sun is hot. We are hungry. We are thirsty. Who should make coffee? Oh well, she would have to pass the kitchen to reach the toilet, anyway…

With her everything was optional. The car ran over the little dog. She could be sad, for it must have felt pain, the poor thing. Did you not hear that last sad whine of death? Let us bury it at the back of the yard. Or she could laugh. The silly little thing. Did you see the way it flew in the air? Did you hear the puny sound that it made? The thing had happened. She had seen it. She had heard it. The little bitch was dead. Really, what did it matter how she responded?

And what really was the difference between lounging, half naked, half drunk, reading poetry between puffs of cigarettes and going down to the slums to dance with the plebs? They're playing Mozart at the theatre. Doris Day's latest musical is at the Odeon. Well…?

'Funny, how things just have a way of happening,' she liked to say, being truthful in her own meaningless way, the words falling from her lips in a tone of helplessness.

'Yes,' I had learned to reply, 'it's funny how things just happen.'

It's a week now since I last saw her. And I suppose I can now understand what happened between us, what ended it all. Of course, I knew as much as she did that it would have to end and perhaps it is silly to ask why. True, things happen. But why so soon, why so abruptly?

She gave the reason, of course, as she had the first night, as she did the last night when I stumbled on her with her skirt above her waist and the youth who had been at the party copulating with her.

'You could at least have gone into the bedroom,' I said before I walked back into the living room. After she had sent the boy away she came back to the living room, lit a cigarette and stared at me. Then she shook her head and said:

'It was so presumptuous of me to have thought for one moment that I would have escaped your contempt, wasn't it?'

'Are you still at that? I don't know what you mean.'

'It's clear what I mean; you despise me, as you despise every-thing else.'

I didn't answer. Only, after a long pause, I went across to her and kissed her. She did not bother to resist. Then I led her into the bedroom, took off her clothes and copulated with her. But it was only with her body. She remained remote, silent and cold. If there was the faintest speck of emotion on her face I suppose it was a vague, empty kind of disappointment.

Then I knew it was finished. For what we had experienced, what had happened between us, was worth happening simply because there was no search for any meaning in it, or any need to explain its termination. It had lingered outside of time, without continuity. There had been no expectation, no expectancy, no hope, no possibility of non-fulfilment. Everything we did was possible, was even enjoyable, simply because of its complete honesty, its total lack of pretentiousness.

It was not just my response after stumbling upon her and the boy on the back veranda which brought things to an end. There were other things I said and did, things I can hardly remember now, but which obviously betrayed my inherent dishonesty. What we experienced could only continue as long as we remained detached, uninvolved, absolutely honest. This came naturally with her, and I suppose what she enjoyed most in me was the fact that for once she had met someone who seemed to have had the same approach. But I'm more human, I suppose, than I had thought. Detachment, with me, can only be the clearing ground for something else; something I want, but do not know of. I sought, despite myself, to place our relationship in time, within meaning, to give it some direction. As it turned out, I only succeeded in making everything cheap, and silly and squalid. I suppose that's what she meant when she said I was contemptuous of her. I'm not sure. Yet it was enjoyable while it lasted. And I do miss those moments with her somewhat.

# PART TWO

## ENTER, THE NOBLE COWARD

> I do shame
> To think of what a noble strain you are,
> And of how coward a spirit.
>
> PERICLES, iv, iii.

# 5

I had to write you, Pauline's letter began, not to plead to you, not with the hope of seeing you again, for that, if you can believe it, is the last thing I should wish for now, but simply because I had to tell someone what I feel, I had to communicate with someone whom I knew would in some way be able to understand, even a little, something of what I wish to express. I know I'm a bore, but before you dismiss me as a sentimental fool, and throw away this letter, please do me the favour of reading on just a little. It may even interest you. There is so much which you don't know, which our very contact, our continued closeness to each other, prevented you from ever knowing about me.

Each evening at about nine I come to the sea by the yacht club, a habit I caught from you. I stare at the sea, at the sky, at the silhouettes of the whites and the light-skinned socialites drinking cocktails in the yacht club. I listen to the gentle prattle of the water as it creeps up to the edge of the road, and then, only then, I feel some sort of peace, some relief from the agony of my loneliness.

There is no need to feel any guilt about this, for you are only indirectly connected with it. You have taken yourself from me and it was the best thing and the worst thing that could have happened to me. Would you be surprised if I told you that I knew all along that this would have happened? That I lived all the while in the knowledge that it would take place at any moment, that it had to take place? And will you shudder with disgust if I say quite frankly that, in one sense, I had a secret longing for it to happen?

You shielded me, Alex. All these years you were the barrier behind which I hid from the world. I lost my identity in you; I gave you everything and made you make me as you wanted me. And why? Because I was afraid. For what other reason? From I was a child I was always afraid. Afraid of Father and Mother; afraid of my sisters and brothers; afraid of those who were not my friends at school and, no less, those who said they were. Afraid of people, afraid of things, afraid of life, of experience.

And as I grew older I grew more afraid. Everything new became a new threat, a new danger to my very existence. In whatever I did, in whatever I said, no matter how trivial, there was the underlying motivation to escape. I had to run, Alex, can you understand this? Always my only thought, my only real need, was to run and hide, to bury my head in the sand.

And then, of course, I met you. I knew all along you never loved me. I knew, as much as you did, that all you felt for me was pity; for you, more than anyone else, had seen through my soul, had seen my fear, my desire to hide. For the first time, really, I was caught naked. No wonder you terrified me so much at first, although, perhaps, you may never have realised this.

And it was because you had exposed me, because you had so easily penetrated all the misty barriers I had created around myself, that I knew I had to have you, or, to be accurate, that you had to have me. What better person to hide behind than you? You, who initially I feared so much.

Can I ever tell you how much I hated myself for it all? I knew the more I leeched myself upon you, the more I became the product of your being, the appendage of your soul, the more pity and responsibility you would feel for me. I knew full well that my total unselfishness towards you was the most unscrupulous form of selfishness. That my abundant kindness was cruel in the guilt it caused you.

I wanted to get away, I wanted to stop, believe me. For, quite apart from using you, I also wanted to love you as I know I should and could love you. But I knew also that this was an idle dream, for to love you I had first to separate myself, and I know that the moment I separated myself I would have lost you. Then I would have lost everything.

So if you haven't already you can cease to feel any guilt for me now. For my grief and my tears are not for you but for the world you have exposed me to once more. Oh, how I want to run away, how I want to flee and hide myself. Now I stand naked, not just before you, but before the whole world. And I am so ashamed. You cannot understand how much I cower and recoil in dread at the confrontation of anything, of anyone.

But there is nowhere to hide; there is nowhere to run to. The city is so small. The island is so small. Everywhere I go I see the same faces, hear the same voices, smell the same air. And their stares and their laughter and their sympathy are all so merciless.

And it's not just the people. Really, they I fear the least. It's the whole ethics of the place, the values, you know what I mean. They terrify me most because they expose me most. For there is nowhere to hide in them. How can I who feel so weak and powerless and shameful, ever hope to hide in something the essence of which is self-mockery? And everything here seems to mock itself either by laughing at itself, or cursing itself. I don't just mean the laughter of the peasants. I don't just mean the sight of two black workers cursing each other about their blackness or even that of a group of brown-skinned upstarts sweating themselves to death drinking tea on a hot afternoon. It's not these particular things, which really are just outward signs of what I do mean. I mean everything taken as a whole, the total impact of the culture. Do I sound a confused fool? I am hoping that you of all persons will be able to understand.

For somehow I think that it was your recognition of what I am trying to identify which began to change you; which gave you the courage to sever yourself from me as you did with everything else connected with it. I suppose the reason why it is so difficult to identify this totality is that in essence it is an absence. What I mean is that it is the feeling that you are facing something which ought to be there but which isn't; or that it is one great sham, a mirage which recedes as you approach it. So often my experience of the values I think I believe in, of life itself, comes to me like a large mysterious present which, with great expectancy, I unwrap, and unwrap and unwrap till I finally discover that a cruel trick has been played on me, that there is nothing there except the garish wrappings.

How am I to know? All I know is that there is no escape to be found here, either in the illusions of the surface, or the vacuum below.

But the main question remains, why, why am I so afraid? Why do I feel my very existence threatened by the confrontation of everything? If I knew the answer to this I would have known everything I want to know. But I can only guess, knowing even before I do that my guesses will all be wrong. One which I have hazarded for some time now is that my fear sprang initially from the closeness, the narrowness, the hopeless provinciality and the shallowness of everything about me. From I was a child I had the terrifying feeling that there was no choice in anything I did; I felt that the world was one great tyrant which ordered every path I took; which made me feel that my actions were the only ones that could have taken place. The older I grew, the greater became this sense of claustrophobia. And the more I felt this way, the greater became my fear of being imprisoned and my need to run and hide. But, of course, I knew very well that there was nowhere to hide, for my fear was caused, in the first place, by the narrowness of everything, the lack of any real choice. My whole life, it seems, has been caught in this vicious circle of fear.

I have explained myself badly, I know, but at least I think you have now some little idea what you meant to me. You can appreciate, if not sympathise, with the reasons why I clung so much to you, refusing to give you the freedom I knew you wanted and needed so much. It was not your love so much I was struggling to keep, Alex, for that I knew deep down I never had; nor was it so much my need to keep on having you to love, for that I also knew was merely a means to an end. I held on to you because I felt that my whole life, my whole existence, depended on it, because I dreaded so much the responsibility of facing up to experience.

And can you blame me? Can you really blame me? All right, so I am a coward. But are we not all cowards? Do we not all seek a way out? Even when, as with you, we choose what appears to be the courageous path of accepting our responsibility for everything, and facing the consequences of our actions, are not these actions themselves a way out? Choice, it seems to me, is an illusion. And so the courage to choose must itself be an illusion. Not that I am denigrating it. It is something even to be admired. But you need faith, a strong invincible faith, to act courageously knowing at the same time that it is an illusion, that in the end you are doomed to cowardice. And faith I lack completely. You, on the other hand, have so much of it, despite what you may say. True, you have changed a great deal, but this you always had and still have. You may not believe in anything now, but I am sure that at least you desperately want to believe in something. I know too that one day you will find whatever it is you want to believe in.

I had leeched myself on you not just to hide, but also, I suppose, with the vain hope that when you did find what you wanted to believe in I would be able somehow to share it with you. How contemptible I am. How right you were to throw me off. If you will pardon the poor imagery, we are all like cacti in the desert of life. The water that nourishes hope and belief is scarce. It is every plant for itself. And there is no place for parasites like me. No place, except perhaps here, beside the reassuring vastness of the sea with its endless motion, below the deep, dark vacancy of the evening sky engulfed in cruel silence.

# 6

Today I walked in the fields at the foot of the mountains. I walked upon the dry leaves of the poinsettias and I can hear them still crumbling beneath my feet. It is still dry and arid. They say a hurricane might come. The news was on the radio all day. And it is strange the reaction of the people to the news. Outwardly the ritual of concern is diligently followed. How terrible! What great misfortune! How many poor wretched lives will be lost? How many years back will our five-year plan be put! Terrible! Terrible! The people all shout. And the priests go on their pulpit and pray to God Almighty to turn the course of tragedy. We have sinned Lord, but…

Yet, at the same time, it is not difficult to detect a strong undercurrent of desire for this storm. Even in the very manner in which intimations of disaster are expressed there is a certain relish. It is a terrible thing, they repeat with sanctimony, but it is the sanctimony of a chain smoker condemning the evils of nicotine. There is joy in tempting destruction. There is joy in desiring destruction. For once I can say I detect a vital unity among my people. For everyone: maidservants and their mistresses; rich men, poor men, black men, white men and most of all brown men; the dwellers of Mona Heights and the dwellers of the shanty towns – all express alike their sweet concern in their own sweet ways. There is a unity in the land at last and all men of goodwill wait with overt dismay, with covert relish, for the coming of the storm.

And I too shared in this delirious expectancy of ruin. Blissfully I walked from the fields into the streets. I stopped to speak to strangers on the wayside. It is so wonderful to be able to confront anyone and share the joys of ruin and desolation with them. 'It veer ten degrees to de right,' the labourer on the roadside said.

Veered ten degrees to the right? I wondered, staring in disbelief at him. What in the name of God does a labourer know about veering ten degrees to the right.

And as if he read my thoughts, he added with undisguised glee, 'That mean it's almost sure to hit us.'

'Good God, no!' I exclaimed.

And he shook his head delightfully and said, 'Yes, yes; it's terrible... but it's coming.'

And I left him and walked further up the road, where I met a sad old peasant who said with sorrow, 'The latest news is that it's turning away and going towards Cuba; isn't that nice?' It was cruel what the storm had done to him, for he was like a tortured man forced to say how wonderful he felt.

Then I went into a barber shop. The barbers had abandoned their scissors; the idlers had given up their dominoes. Men, women and children were crammed together around the little radio set. Not even the cricket commentary of a Test match could have stimulated the tense excitement on their faces.

Then came the bulletin. Alas, the storm had moved even further away; it was almost certain to hit the Dominican Republic, but it was doubtful whether it would change its course so radically that it could hit Jamaica. But keep your ears tuned to the radio, the announcer offered. You never know.

'Thank God,' a young tart in the corner said naively. No one even bothered to look at her. A wise, emaciated old man, who, from his appearance, had obviously weathered many a storm, offered a few rays of hope.

'In nineteen-fifty-one they said the same thing; no one expect it to come; the radio said it wouldn't come; and you remember what happened? You 'member 'ow de whole of West Kingston wipe clean; you 'member 'ow de water from de gully flood de place and wash 'way all of Gordon Town; you 'member?...'

And there were other tales of other storms; luscious, gruesome tales of pregnant women lanced through the belly with missiles of steel fencing uprooted miles away; of ceilings falling in and crushing families to pulp; of churches tumbling down – strange how it was that the churches always get the worse hit, strange how it was.

But after all the tales were told and all the possibilities explored there was still the dismal doubt that it might not come after all.

'Thank God,' the tart in the corner dared again, this time more loudly. We stared at her with sheepish eyes and nodded our agreement grudgingly. But it was clear from our countenances that we all felt to choke her. She was obviously imposing a subtle form of moral blackmail on us. We all knew that our expressions of relief were insincere. But the empathy of the little crowd we formed demanded such insincerity. And in our own perverse way we were all intensely sincere in our insincerity. Yet this whore, this little smelly tart, unbalanced everything – the unity, the syntality, the sweet indulgence of our need for destruction – by her insistence on thanking God. And she had us all cornered, for sanity, which as yet we had not completely thrown off, obliged us to agree with her. So we were caught out by this whore between the pedestrian trappings of our conventional ethic and this new, blissful state of viscosity which transcended sanity, which in essence was nothing less than the expression of our latent desire for dissolution. Oh how we hated her!

Then came another bulletin to settle the matter finally. The storm had definitely turned away. There was no possibility of it hitting the island again. The danger was over. There would not even be another bulletin.

We stood agape in the barber shop, staring in silence at each other, deflated, flattened, crushed. In a moment everything was gone: the joy of expectancy, the unity, the empathy. We were just ordinary people in a crummy old barber shop again, devoid of all hope, condemned once again to the barren monotony of the absence of all danger. In that moment of deflation, at that point just before we hit the ground of drab sanity once again, I think we all had a sudden shock of revelation. We saw everything within us which we had made bearable by taking completely for granted. For we suddenly saw ourselves for what we all were: grains of sand on the black shore; trees in a nameless forest; faces in a little crowd. We had nothing to hope for. Nothing to look forward to except another kinky head of hair to trim, another road to pave, another minute to file away, another game of dominoes. We all felt in that cruel moment how ordinary we were, how drab we were, how sane and unexciting we all were.

Then the awful silence was broken by the same whore in the corner, who piped up a third time: 'Thank God! Thank God!' But this time she had gone too far. The barber turned upon her in rage and shouted:

'You nasty little bitch: shut up! shut up! As a matter of fact, get your ass out of my shop; get out!'

It was a cry of anguish and we all shared it with him, even if the majority of us had returned enough to our senses not to say a word. The whore left with her head hanging down, and after that, bedraggled and sad, we followed her quietly out.

I stood outside for a moment, then turned round and went back into the barber shop. I am not quite sure why I did that, partly, I suppose, to recapture something of what I had experienced with the little crowd not so long before. I stared at the barber, who, with his hammer, was pulling down the wind barriers he had nailed across the window. I watched him till he was through, sharing his disappointment with him. When he had finished he turned round and for a moment we stared at each other. Then he looked down at the pieces of board he held in his hands across his chest with the mildly frustrated expression of someone who had been left holding the baby.

'Such a goddamn waste of time,' he grumbled wearily.

'Did you know,' I offered consolingly, 'that at the heart of the hurricane there is only a vacuum?'

Without replying he walked to the back door and flung the planks away.

# 7

Today I drifted to the marketplace. I wandered idly among the people. Among the screaming higglers and fat peasant women with their oily black skin who smelt of yams and cocos and coconut oil and the other things of the earth. Among the vegetables, the black-eyed peas, green bananas, sweet potatoes and trash-heaps which smelt of the sweat of the higglers and the peasant women and the other things of the earth.

I rubbed shoulders with the buyers and I haggled with the sellers. There were many ladies of good breeding there, brown ladies, pink ladies and even nice black ladies, all with their haggard, reluctant housemaids struggling behind them with huge baskets filled with the fat of the land.

I wandered in the noise, the great, perpetual din of the city in the marketplace. I heard a hundred times the harsh sarcasm of their laughter, the dry wit of their tongue, the vitriolic outbursts of their curses.

There were many young men, too, in the market-place, smoothly dressed in gabardine trousers and well-pressed white shirts with the cuffs meticulously turned up twice. Those were the men to watch, said the wise old higgler to her olive-shaded customer. Do not be fooled by their wide, bland look of innocence. They are sly brutes and their hands are fast and they will steal the very milk from your cup of coffee.

There were hordes of children in the marketplace, Meagre, ragged entrails, with oversized bellies and exposed buttocks. Like the lilies of the field and the birds of the air they seem hardly to care for the next moment, much less for the morrow. They ran about the market-place, disturbing the delicately constructed pyramids of yams, cursing, cursed at, laughing, laughed at. For there was much food to be had in the market; though sometimes there would be screams of fear as they were dragged to the jailhouse by the Special Constables.

And there were older men with beards who all stood aloof. A part of the horde, yet away from it all. These wise men spoke incessantly, and with great reverence, of another land called Ethiopia, that same place which the heathens called Africa, where all was bliss and peace and love. Where the nastiness, the greed, the suffering, the cheap, maddening indignity of the marketplace, did not exist.

They were half-naked, these tall black men with their beards and long, woolly braids of unkempt hair, with the other half of their bodies clothed in rags. But they held themselves upright with a dignity that silently mocked the squalor, the subservience, the displaced aggression of the marketplace. They spoke with such reverence and good faith that their prophesies took on meaning beyond the mere utterance of their words. The meaning of decency, I suppose, of pride regained, of deep conviction.

So I went up to one of these cultists and I asked him with humility what was to be, what was to come of us who did not believe. And he drew himself up and he said with great wrath:

'Thou shall burn, Babylon; oh you son of Sodom; you who was mothered in whoredom and villainy; if you are not with us, then you are against us; an' if you are against us then you shall surely suffer the dreadful fate of the oppressors. Your tongue shall be plucked out! You shall be made to thirst until the verge of death with a glass of cold lemonade dangling less than an inch from your lips. Then you shall be roasted slowly from the big toes upwards. There will be no mercy; no mercy whatever for the oppressors of the children of the black God, the children of slavery, the true Israelites!'

'Are you a Jew, then?' I asked him timidly.

He took a deep breath and was on the point of belching his holy wrath on me again when another, much older, locksman interrupted him.

'Hold your tongue, brother,' he commanded. 'Peace an' love.' And as the other held his peace, the older man looked straight at me, into me, beyond me, with his large murky brown eyes, and he said:

'We are all Jews lost in the wilderness, brother, and we are all black men, according to the Word. And the Word, which is the Truth, say unto I: In this world, in this life, every man is a Jew searching for his Zion; every man is a black man lost in a white world of grief.'

After I left the marketplace something terrible happened to me. I went to bathe for the first time at a deserted beach called Green Bay. I drove to the foot of the hill on the other side of which was the bay. Then I walked up a narrow, stony path winding its way for a half-mile or so till I reached the top of the hill. I looked over the trees and could just see the blue face of the water grinning at me through the leaves. Enticed, I scrambled down until I reached a sharp bend in the path and, going round it, I suddenly came face to face with the wide, quiet grandeur of the ocean. The confrontation was at first wonderful, overwhelming. I felt like a bedraggled Columbus: tired, lost, on the verge of giving up, suddenly seeing his new world. It was mine, this great, silent thing. I felt I was the first to see it, the first to smell it, the first to fully experience it. The eyes of others had no doubt fallen on it before. Perhaps they had even dared to bathe in it. But I, I was the first to feel it in this way. I was the first to whom it had such meaning, such sanctity.

It was its silence that impressed me most, for I could not yet hear the breaking of the waves on the white shore. It was the direct opposite of the city, which was so small, so jumbled, so squalid, so noisy. Now I was confronted with an unending vastness which was pure, clean and unruffled. Mesmerised, I stood where I was and stared with my mouth open. Then slowly I began to walk down the rest of the other side of the hill until I reached the shore.

I stopped somewhere on the middle of the shore. I was alone. More and more this simple fact grew upon me. I was alone. And the more my sense of loneliness grew, the more I began to feel a delicious sense of fear growing in me. Like a fool, I gave in to this fear, some sixth sense warning me of the danger. Then I reached the point where I had to make the great choice of total submission or complete withdrawal. Like someone who had taken an over-dose of sleeping tablets and had been woken up on the point of death faced with the choice of remaining awake and living or giving in to the sweet compulsion of perpetual sleep, I struggled a little, wavered, then gave in.

In my submission I not only saw but felt, felt deep-deep, in my head, in my heart, in my testicles, in my bones, the essence of everything about me, of everything. The sweeping, overwhelming, yet compressed grandeur of everything. All was a stark arc-like sweep. A vast basin with the greater portion of its side cut away through which the sea, coming from somewhere in eternity, emptied itself. Facing the great water the mountain over which I had just climbed rose on my left, then swept away horizontally behind me, then came back round on my right; vertically as well, curving upwards above me then down, ending in an angle of forbidding water-locked rocks and boulders.

The surface of this mountain, stark and bare except for the austere cacti and aged thorn trees, the rocks and the pebbles and the centuries old seashells, also sunk away in a concavity from me.

I walked vacantly about the shore, soiling the white sand with my feet. It was soft and fine and moist. More and more the disquieting urge grew to dig a deep hole somewhere in it and bury myself there. For by now my fear was no longer something I could exteriorise; no longer something to feel, or dread or desire or resent. It had become me, the thing that I was. It had crept into my blood, into my veins. It was the current that kept me alive, conscious of what I was. It was the assumption of my being, so it was no longer possible to question it; only at times to have sudden intimations of it in little treacherous shocks of confrontation.

Like those things there on the beach, those unnamed things washed up by the sea. A coconut bough? Was that once the foot of a chair? A piece of shingle? An oar? Branches of what were once trees? Pieces of female undergarments? All of them still had their pathetic pretensions to uniqueness. But they were all so cruelly the same. They had all lived the life of the sea, had all felt its silent, consuming force, had all been metamorphosed into sameness and inanimation. Washed up. Dead.

Yet their inanimation only emphasised for me something

more terrifying. A terror which was life itself and which confronted me fully in the stark grandeur of the bay. So that I felt that nature itself had now betrayed me. I had come here quite shamelessly to escape, to escape everything in which I could in any way detect an extension of myself: those others; and the houses and the streets, and the movements and the sounds. I had come here to seek in the commanding quietude of the ocean, as I had always sought, the moment of dissolution, the sweet delirious separation from all that would become me, the passing away from time, space, feeling and from thought.

But not today. For instead there was this:

The great water. The water that flowed from the sea into the sand. The sand that flowed from the beach into the gaping abyss of the sky. The sky that continued the sweeping complexity of arcs over into the horizon, into the sea again.

I stared at the water at the foot of the horizon and saw that it was black. Then as it came towards me, with its calm, stealthy, incomprehensible power, I see that its colour began to change to a dark green. Nearer and it was light green. Then it was only a few yards from the beach on which I stood and it was crystal clear, melting again into the sand, which dissolved once more into the mountain, which interlocked with the sky, which...

Then slowly, but with agonising certainty, the thing which faced it began to realise, however dimly, that it was being trapped. For the motion of the arcs was gathering pace till the whole universe had formed one vast gigantic circle. And it was lost there in the centre of it.

The thing's fears grew worse as it turned round and round, stupidly trying to separate the end from the beginning till it finally realised with great terror that there was neither end nor beginning. Then it was that it knew it had to escape somehow.

But it was far, far too late. How could it? Where could it run to? Where could it hide? In the sea? In that water which threatened to engulf everything? In this sand, which threatened to choke everything? Among those cacti, which threatened to bludgeon everything?

Nothing was possible. There was no escape. For they were all the same. The sea, the sand, the mountain, the sky and the horizon, they were all absolutely identical. They had all merged into one vast, abysmal circle, going round and round with it inside. Head began to reel and there was the realisation that it went round with the motion of the circle, faster and yet faster. It was at the mercy of the motion of everything.

Then came the final agony. For a brief instant my head cleared. I became totally aware, my senses no longer numb. Consciousness came like a flash of lightning in the darkness of hell and I now knew with absolute certainty that the circle around me was growing smaller and smaller. And the faster it spun, the smaller I became.

It was then that the screaming began. What was odd was that the screaming seemed to be coming from afar, detached from myself, as if my response, my physical terror, had separated itself from me. But it must have been my screaming. It must have been my voice, my response. I know that the only proof I have that this was so was the fact that I was alone, therefore the cry of anguish could only have come from me. And of my loneliness I am absolutely certain.

It was I who screamed. It must have been, for I could feel the water creeping up on me, its millions of frothy white claws coming nearer and nearer, pieces even falling off and touching me. And where it touched it melted through my flesh and my bones like acid. And the cacti with its thorns had also begun to fall from off the mountain, sticking and raking me. Then the mountain began to crumble. The sky caved in. And as everything came closer and closer upon me the only sound I could hear was a deep, fierce hum which came to me as if I was lost, naked in the middle of a hive of monster bees.

Then I began to cower. Flat out on my belly with my face in the sand I begged and I pleaded for mercy. But when, for the last time, I took a fleeting glance up, I found that everything had almost sunk into itself, and I was on the verge of being crushed to pulp.

Then I felt the hand of the fisherman, holding me tightly, shaking me. 'Take it easy; control yourself, man,' I heard him saying. He had a tall, handsome black figure with large honest eyes. I found myself panting, and held my head, which felt swollen and was vibrating with pain. As I came to my senses I began to feel a little foolish and mumbled something to him about a sunstroke. He and his friend took me to their canoe and rowed me across the bay to their hut. I was put to lay down on a broad plank cushioned with banana trash which was their bed. His woman rubbed my head with bay-rum and afterwards she gave me some mint tea to drink. Then, against their protestations, I thanked them and I left, though even now I am still dazed, and still a little scared.

## 8

Consciousness dawned upon me slowly, like tears swelling up. I am still slightly bewildered, slightly dazed. All this morning I had simply drifted about the city. I had spent the night with a whore, who woke me up at five in the morning and said it was time to go. Without a word I dressed and left.

When I went outside the fresh morning air hit my face and I shivered a little in the chill of the morning dew. On my left the lane went down to the waterfront, on my right up to one of the main streets leading to the Parade. I stood in front of the gate of the brothel for about five minutes, chilled with indecision, not knowing where to turn, not wanting to go anywhere. Eventually I saw a human figure on the main road to my right and so I decided to take the opposite direction where the only thing in sight was a sore-infested mongrel ransacking the garbage cans.

Slowly I walked down the little lane with the quiet little hovels close on either side of me. There was a beauty in the fresh, moist quiet of the dawn which permeated even the hovels about me. It was hard to believe then that in every one of them human things were packed from wall to wall beside each other, or more likely on top of each other.

In the silence of the dawn I realised how much of this ugly, barren city was sheer noise. A rolling, empty barrel which sputtered and roared and squeaked with the moans of hunger, the spite of resentment, the whines of greed, the lies of deception, the sighs of resignation.

How beautiful everything was now in the stillness. The harsh angles of the little huts, patched together from the sides of empty barrels, were now smoothed out with the moisture of the dew. I felt I was thrown back into time, walking alone on the streets of the relic of some ancient city. As I walked down the narrow lane I created fantasies of a real past.

What ancient civilisation flourished here long, long ago? How clever and resourceful they must have been to have made houses as durable as these out of the sides of empty codfish barrels. Who were the men that ruled them? Were they of another race, of another culture? How great and ingenious they must have been to create a mosaic of streets such as these. And in the same grid pattern as the Romans, too. Look, there are even gutters, part of their elaborate drainage system. I wonder what kind of refuse these gutters drained away? The waters of how many Rabelaisian baths; the vomit of how many sumptuous feasts?

There is a past here. There must be a past here. My city goes back a thousand years. If you dig deep you will find the relics of even more ancient times. They tell me that all I would find are the twisted bones of crippled, mutilated black slaves, or, if I dig deeper, the decapitated bodies of Arawak Indians whose heads were chopped off in sport by Spanish settlers or left half eaten by the Caribs before them. But they are all lies, lies. I will not believe them. They could show me a million musty documents. Those curators of the British Museum, the Public Records Office, the Institute of Jamaica and the Archives of Spanish Town, they are all vile, treacherous, scheming propagandists, brainwashers, inventors of fables designed to make me feel inferior, to deprive me of the knowledge of my glorious heritage, which must be there, hidden somewhere.

For it is not possible, it cannot be, that all there is, that all there ever was, are the harsh sounds of the cracking of cart-whips, the vile curses of cruel, inhuman masters, the rhythm of steel hoes plunging into unyielding, virgin soil. And what have they done to my great, immortal works of art? Is that all? Am I to believe that all I have inherited are these dry, sardonic melodies with their harsh, melancholic refrains?

I shall not believe them. One day I shall destroy those evil institutes with their corridors and shelves of lies, and I shall burn them to the ground. I, Alexander Blackman, shall redeem the truth of my heritage, of my great past, that lies hidden somewhere.

Here, even in these streets of the morning dew, perhaps. There is still no sound. The only change so far has been a slight brilliance on the skyline to the east. I have found it, then, the streets and the houses of my ancient city.

At the end of the street I stood facing the waterfront. A great, long white ship was docked in the harbour, the sea around it a motionless, greenish-black glacier.

Still nothing moved, nothing changed except the skyline on the eastern horizon. It was growing brighter and brighter. I had a premonition that at any moment something would erupt on that eastern horizon. And whatever it would be I instinctively feared it. For I knew, I felt with absolute certainty, that that sudden change in the eastern skyline would disrupt the sudden peace and solace that I had found in the quiet of the morning, in the sacred past of my little city.

So I hurried back into the maze of little lanes, hoping that I would lose myself there, that I would be spared the agony of confronting what was bound to happen soon in the eastern part of the sky.

But as I walked the morning crept more and more upon me. The thing in the east kept following me, wherever I went. I sought out the narrowest lanes, the darkest corners, but the light grew brighter and brighter, everywhere about me.

Then suddenly, having teased and taunted me, the sky in the east exploded. I stood at the dead-end of an alley and, powerless, felt the rising sun. Then all too soon everything was gone. The dew, with its soft, moist, comforting smugness, suddenly vanished. The crepuscular cloak of dawn evaporated, leaving the sides and the fronts and the tops of the little hovels exposed. Naked in their slovenliness; ugly and smeared in their squalid patchiness.

The transient, dreamlike beauty of the dawn was gone. And my past went with it; my little ancient city went with it; my peace and my pride went with it. Now I had to face the truth of the new day; the harsh reality of the cruel sun. Perhaps it would soon go away again, perhaps…

But then I heard the loud, tired yawn of a whore coming from within the hovels; I heard the obscene laughter of her satiated client; I heard her vile, angry retort. I walked quickly away, my hand covering my ears like a madman. But it couldn't keep out the loud shrieks of a hungry baby which suddenly crashed into the morning. Slowly, I took my hand away from my ears, daring myself to identify the origin of the cry. But I couldn't, for at times it seemed to come from afar, at other times it seemed to be coming from the hut on the right side of the road, at other times it made me jump with fright as it seemed to be coming from the window immediately to my left. For a moment it seemed that the whole damn' world was full with the cry of hungry babies; yes, and it was coming up from the very earth beneath me. I placed my hand upon my ears once more and began to run. I ran and ran between the narrow streets, bouncing upon garbage men, falling over the carcasses of rotting dogs, slipping on the slime of the gutters and falling with my face squashed upon the asphalt. Then when I could run no more I collapsed on the sidewalk in front of a rum-bar, on one side of which was a sound-system dance hall and on the other a brothel called 'Paradise'.

So it was for real, then. And it was for now. People were actually inside there, behind those decaying patches of wood. They were doing things behind there; all sorts of things. I had been deceived by the dawn. I had been mocked by the dawn. See them there. They are beginning to crawl out of their shelters. They are real people; living things. True I can see their skeletons, but there is nothing of the past about their eyes. They are as of now. Everything is as of now.

I heard the rising din of the city. And I saw that they had opened the rum-bar. So I went inside.

# 9

...after tearing up Elaine's letter I lay on my back on the bed in the room of the Hall of Residence which I had rented from the university, and fell into a dazed half-sleep. Then, in a kind of conscious dream, I saw myself as the child I once was. I was walking barefooted in short trousers in the streets of the little village. I walked with a bemused frown on my face from street to street. But was that all? There must have been something there in those childhood days that is worth remembering. I forced myself to remember.

I played cricket, lots of cricket. We used to quarrel and fight over whose turn it was to bat, or whether one of us had been caught leg-before-wicket or not. Yes, and I remember forcefully that the argument was always settled by the boy who was the umpire, and those who were on his side, insisting that 'the umpire's decision is final!' It was said with a certain sanctity, as if it had all the force of moral law behind it. I was never quite sure about that remark. There was something very odd about it. For one thing, it was always expressed in proper English; and then again, it was said in that tone, that assertive, absolute tone, which was so alien to the moral chaos of our ordinary behaviour. And I suppose it was the oddity of this expression which made us, in the end, all obey it.

But quite apart from this alien expression, there is nothing else I can remember about those games. Not the friends I used to play with; nor even how I felt, in any particular way, about the game. I simply liked to play it, that is all.

And there is little else I could recall in my semi-dream. All I could see was myself walking, walking, through the lanes, up the hills, to the wretched school.

Ah yes, I had a friend. His name was William, just William. William? But he was not real. He was the hero of the books I used to read. Yet I do remember him more vividly than any living acquaintance I had. I remember that I never quite understood him. He lived in a strange land; he went to boarding school; he spoke a kind of English which I associated more with my teachers, and this confused me no end, for I am sure William was my friend. But he was such a distant friend; so remote. Sometimes I think he never realised I even existed. So I had to make him know that I existed. After all, it was only fair; I spent so much time with him.

So I often wrote William letters. I told him what a naughty, selfish brat I thought he was. Not because he had a father, and he could afford to wear shoes and socks all the time, and his parents were better off than mine, and he was English; not because of all this did he think he could behave like that with me. I told him, too, to stop speaking the way he did, for, in a close friend of mine, I found it most disturbing. And I told him that for a boy of ten he sometimes asked the silliest questions. Really, there was no need to embarrass his elder brother in that manner. Didn't he know all about sex, and what big people did?

I placed my letters in envelopes and addressed them to 'Just William; England'. I gave them to my mother, who posted them for me. But I never received any reply.

Am I to believe that that was all? What of the songs I used to sing? Yes, what of them: 'All Through the Night', 'Early One Morning', 'The Blue Bells of Scotland'. Dreaming back now, I can't with any honesty say that I did not like those songs. Nor can I say that they presented any kind of problems. In fact, I loved those Celtic melodies; they are among the few pleasant memories I have of that sadistic institution which they call school here. But the fact cannot be denied that they were songs about Wales, about Scotland, about England. They spoke of maidens and fair shepherdesses, of rolling hills and plains, of manners and folkways of which I knew virtually nothing. So it was only possible to love these songs by dissociating myself from their content. Meaning had to be deprived of all substance. These songs could only be beautiful and moving and memorable by selecting only their form; only their style and their melodies. So like all my other memories these traced their steps back to abrupt dead-ends. Memory becomes the vehicle merely for the empty shells of melodies; for the recollection of a friend who never existed; for the odd, blindly obeyed commands of a game I used to play; for a child who used to walk from street to street and dream of other places; of friends he did not know; of heroes he did not understand, of the adult he would one day become, the adult whom he is now, who dreams vainly of the boy he once was, who used to dream, so much…

However, there was one real thing, one living being who stood outside of this crazy unreal circle, his mother. He put away his diary and stood up, startled. It was amazing that he had not thought of her before. For she was always there. She was there from the very beginning. She created him in her womb. She nursed him; she clothed him; she protected him. She was always there, and she was still there, a solid, living, real link between what he used to be and what he was now; an unceasing, ever-present observer on his process of becoming.

Suddenly he was filled with the urge to confront her, to touch her, to hold her tightly to him. He would tell her, the only living relic of his past, how much he loved her. He would ask her, and in asking her ask his past to forgive him for his neglect, for his cold detachment. Through her he would recreate the past. Through her he would make it something meaningful. Through her he would give it content, give it substance. Those songs will be made to mean something, if not other songs would be found. His own folksongs – 'Brown Skin Gal', 'Linstead Market', Peel Head John-Crow', 'Solas Market' – which he had learned to think of as silly peasant prattle, these he would sing with her. She would remind him of the friends he used to have and the things they used to do; she would remind him of the places he used to go and what he had thought of them. He would make her tell him stories – stories of Anancy, the spider man, which her mother had told her, which she should have told him, but never had the time to. She would tell him stories of the stories he used to tell her. For, like all children, he must have heard some, and must have come to her and told her of them; and there must have been times when she was not too busy to have listened.

He changed his clothes hurriedly, then dashed outside. It could not have been later than four in the afternoon. All he could think of as he hastened to the bus-stop was the anticipated joy of their reconciliation. This barrier which had grown up between them would be broken down. This was a journey of rediscovery – that of the lost dream of his childhood. This was a journey back to the very womb. A re-digging of the earth of his life. A replanting of roots.

It was a hot afternoon and he became drenched with perspiration as he hurried to the market-square where he would catch the bus. When he reached the bus-stop he found a large crowd waiting for the bus. They were mainly higglers and market women down from the countryside going to the city. At first he thought of going back to the campus and borrowing a car, but on second thought he decided to remain with the crowd. For at last he began to feel that somehow he belonged to this crowd. They were his people, the common possessors of his new-found past. Everyone of those shouting, bustling stout peasant women was his mother. And how he needed their affection; how he needed their warmth; how responsible he felt to them.

The large grey bus had arrived. The door opened, and then the mad rush to get in started. The haggard, scowling conductress shouted, more in the performance of a kind of ritual of protest than in earnest, that they form a queue. They neglected her and hustled in.

Standing at the back of the crowd, Alexander smiled indulgently. He could witness this uproar all day. He could wallow in their full-blooded gusto without end. Suddenly, overwhelmed with their wonderful animation, he plunged into the crowd himself. He pushed and he bounced and he jeered and he laughed and he swore. He lost himself completely in the oneness of their violence until suddenly, quite exhausted, he found himself squashed upon a seat near the back of the bus amid the baskets and crocus bags and boxes of foods.

His eyes fell upon an old woman struggling through the door, half laughing, half angry. He watched her carefully as she made her way to the back of the bus, rubbed the leather of the seat and stroked it three times, then sat down, making a deep, earthy moan of pleasure: 'Lawd,' she said, with a dry, mischievous humour, 'back into the kitchen!' Her skin was black and shrivelled. But the veins on her neck stood out defiantly. Her body was spare, but seemed well oiled and seasoned with the sweat of age, so that you felt that in another hundred years she would look very much the same. He wondered who she was, what special cares she had, what special griefs. Then her eyes caught his. A look of surprise overcame her. She looked on either side of her, then down on herself to see if anything was wrong. Then she glanced suspiciously back at Alex. Soon her suspicion turned to sheer annoyance.

'Wait a minute,' he heard her grumbling, 'wait, wait, wait…' Alex looked away, not a little embarrassed.

He got off the bus at the end of the Mountain View Road on the eastern side of the city. Then he ran without stopping towards his mother's home, hoping that she would have returned from the shop by then. He opened the front door and stood, choked with excitement, in the living room. Then he shouted: 'Mother!'

He had never called her 'Mother!' before. Until he was ten, in fact, he had been brought up to believe that his mother was his elder sister and had called his grandmother 'mamma'. Only when she had died was he told the truth. It had come as no shock. He had always suspected that there was something more than sisterly in her relationship with him. Yet he had found it difficult transferring the term 'mamma' to her. He had felt somehow silly saying it, and was always left a little flushed afterwards. A compromise had finally been arrived at by the use of the term 'mam', which could, from the ambiguous pronunciation he gave it, be interpreted either as 'ma'am' or as 'mum'.

He had received no reply and so he called again. This time the term 'Mother' did jar rather a bit. Suddenly he heard the back door open. She was in. She was coming.

They met in the hallway joining the living and dining rooms. When she saw his expression she became apprehensive.

'Something wrong? What happen?'

'Nothing; nothing in particular,' he assured her.

'Then why do you come so suddenly. I've never seen you at this time of …'

'Mother, I want to talk to you. There is so much we have to say to one another.'

He took her hand and led her back into the living room. She remained perplexed and anxious. After sitting down he began:

'Nothing is wrong, except… except what I have caused to come between us. I have been so cruel, so insensitive. I took you so much for granted, you of all people, that I forgot that you had deep feelings too; I forgot that you are the only person I could be sure really loved me, since you cannot help but love me. I have been… I have created this barrier…'

The words faded away on his lips. He thought of what he had just said, of the situation he was in, and felt a perfect fool. He recoiled in self-embarrassment at the sheer artificiality and insincerity of what he had brought himself into.

But it was too late. He had touched her where she was most sensitive; had let loose a well of restrained feelings. As long as he had remained aloof, apart from her, without any gesture of reconciliation, she could afford to keep back the sorrow, the grief, the disappointment that had grown so deeply in her. Now at last he had showed some signs of return, of being in some little way the person she knew him once to be. So all she could do was burst into tears. Tears for his cruelty, tears for his separation, tears for the joy of having him again.

And the more she wept, the more he silently cursed himself for the hypocritical fool he was. He had begun an act. The cue had been given. Now he was forced to continue the false play and reciprocate. But he had nothing to say. There was really nothing he could say. If he continued in the same vein, prolonging the act, for her sake, to its end of apparent reunion, he would despise himself for the mockery he had made of her. On the other hand, it was impossible now to confess the truth to her. How could he tell her that it was all a mad urge to make his past meaningful? What kind of a joke would she think he was playing with her? And how was it possible to deny that he did love her, that he did need her? At least in the silence that had crept between them there was always the possibility of hoping; she could always pray to her God with the hope that there would be an answer.

Now, in his shameful rashness, he had committed himself to words; and words had trapped him into insincerity from which there was no retreat except into guilt.

So guilt he chose. He accepted that he had been cruel to her, that he had been merciless. To his mother; the person to whom he owed so much. He was guilty. He was responsible for her tears, for the anguish she now expressed.

In this manner he found it possible to put his hand on her shoulder and say, with some sincerity, that he was sorry. She acknowledged his gesture, thinking he was still speaking about his separation from her and his desire for reunion. He tried to tell himself that this was not how she had interpreted his last gesture; that she knew he was talking about the fool he had made of her. But he knew she had had no way of knowing this and that in fact all he had done was to deceive her further.

So now he felt guilty about his guilt, which, on the level he had first sought to meet it, could not possibly have been real. And he felt remorse, too, at the insincerity of the deceitful manner in which he had made it possible to tell her, with some sincerity, that he was sorry.

Suddenly he smashed his palms in his face and moaned with contrition. His mother came up close to him and placed her arms around him. He recoiled in horror and self-revulsion at her touch, but she held on firmly to him.

'Don't blame yourself too much,' she said forgivingly, 'don't be too hard on yourself. I'm all right now. I have you again. You are my son again. My son.'

Her voice trailed out as she said the last word in a spasm of joy. He was crippled into silence as she pressed her cheeks against his and the salt of her tears creased his lips. He could only sit there beside her, petrified, his eyes staring with horror and shame, inwards, upon himself.

## 10

I have remained locked up in my room all day. In a half-drunken stupor, I keep falling into sleep which at first is calm but gradually becomes more troubled with all sorts of crazy nightmares. One recurring dream I have is that of climbing with a group of silent, gaunt, stiff people up an incredibly long spiral stairway. We keep going up and up, around and around, the top never seeming to come. Every turn I make I seem to think that we have reached, for they would slow down a little, but as it turns out the pace has been reduced simply to adjust to the ever-increasing narrowness of the stairway. I never see their faces, only their straight, forbidding wooden backs, for I struggle on several paces behind the last of them. Then suddenly, when I have given up hope of ever reaching anywhere, they all stop and then go into a room. I only have a brief glimpse of the room from where I stand below and I observe that the walls are bare concrete and it seems to be empty for the murmuring which begins when they enter sounds hollow and distant. Then it is my turn to enter the room and it is only then that I notice that between the last stair and the doorway was an open space and I stand there, frozen, gazing with dread down at the vast emptiness below me. I do not know how they managed to get in for they all appear to do it effortlessly. I try everything, I think of every way, to get in too. For this I am certain of – I did want to get inside. I do not know why I want to, for really the people in there do not interest me very much with their strange ethereal whisperings. I simply feel compelled to enter. I know too that there is no going back. Not down those narrow stairs. Not by myself alone. But how can I enter? I realise that it was my fear, my ever-increasing horror of falling into the abyss, which prevents me from entering. For I can easily jump across. I can even do what they all did, they who were not afraid, that is, simply take one long, fearless stride across.

But I could only stand there, frozen in anguish; unable to go back, unable to go forward, petrified in my confrontation with my desire to enter the open door and my fear of falling into the deep, dark abyss. And it was at that point, always, that I woke up, drenched in the sweat of my fear.

It is now six o'clock. Is it morning? Is it evening? Anyway, it hardly matters. I am so acutely lonely. It has never been quite like this before. Now there seems no longer even the possibility of self-deception. Everything about me – that wall there, that chair, that little narrow bed, that basin of stale water – seem so aloof. They seem to stand away. In another place. In another time. Now is only me. And there are the voices of the students next door. Their laughter. I listen to them. I try to hear what they are saying, but they seem to make no sense. There is no meaning in words any more. Their voices come to me like a half-forgotten melody that revives some distant, childhood dream. The very closeness of their voices seems to push me back, away from itself, from them, into some long forgotten time. I am on the other side of some vague eternity from them, from everything.

Now, finally, that which I am, has trapped me, has cut me off. I am conscious of that table so I am not that table. It means nothing to me; it never can mean anything to me. I am conscious of those others next door, so I am not them. Of thought, so I do not think. Of consciousness, so I can hardly be said to be conscious. All that there is, is some vague sensing of having been. My awareness comes upon me as something having past, an ever-passing presence, always an agonising step behind something else. I was. I wanted to be. To be anything – them next door, that wall, even. Yet my every effort wanting to be only throws me more upon the thing I am, the active recollection which evades me; only intensified the immediate past that I was; only makes me more aware of the self that I am always losing.

I must find an excuse for all this. Something in me, something painful, something engulfing, something compelling, forces me

115

to bridge the gap, to justify the separation of this thing which can only recollect, from everything else.

Well, let me at least pretend to try. There is race. There is society. There is history. Must I grasp the excuses that they offer? Must I declare aloud that I belong to the dispossessed of the earth? Must I shout all that consummate shit about how they've stolen my golden Africa with its empires which they tried to cover up; must I plead the slavery of my ancestors; must I declare the incoherent shambles which is the culture of my country? But what has all this to do with me? What has history, what have all those musty, moth-eaten manuscripts and travellers' accounts, got to do with me, me, this thing here that lives? What have Ashanti warriors, with their golden stool and ceremonies and God knows what, got to do with me, me, this living thing that sits upon its wooden stool? So what if they have beaten my ancestors to death? What have those masters to do with me? What have the descendants of those masters to do with me, me, this thing that lives? And what do I know about culture? What do I care about culture? How can a concept, a thought, the erudite abstraction of other men's minds, have any real meaning for me, me, this single, concrete thing that lives, that comes before everything?

There is always Mother, of course. And there is always the father that never was. Oedipus and all that. Have I not done that woman enough harm? I have made her suffer. Part of me is the guilt I feel for her. And must she now be transformed into some hifaluting concept, some meaningless excuse? I left her womb thirty years ago. Here I am now, a separate thing whom she hardly knows. What has she got to do with this, this thing here, me, upon this stool, writing, yearning?

No, there is no longer any excuse, any reason, any explanation to be found outside myself. I come before history, I come before race, I come before culture, I come before parents, I come before God. At this point the very effort of finding such excuses has become mockingly self-defeating. In doing so I am like a temporarily impotent man straddled over a voluptuous, naked woman, incapable of having an erection, forcing myself to have one, while making humiliating excuses to her, yet by this very effort, by this very attempt at explaining his incapacity, failing even more.

There are no excuses to be found. There are no explanations outside of the thing which lives, which always was. All that I know is that I was, that I am ever passing, that I am always on the point of catching up with myself, the thing that lives, the moment now. But always it seems too late. Always I keep yearning to be what I am, but never was.

Suddenly he could write no more. He flung his diary from him in disgust and got up. Something had to be done. He couldn't continue like this. His thoughts, his feelings, his entire being had arrived at a dead end and it was no longer possible to evade the fact. He would act. Some decision had to be made, some final plunge taken.

And the only one which both reason and emotion demanded was an end to everything. It was quite clear that there was no point going on any more. Suicide was the only answer. He would drown himself. He had always feared and been fascinated by the idea of drowning, of being swallowed by the ocean; and he would do so now. There was no longer any point in asking why. The time for such asking had already passed. The act of suicide was self-explanatory. He felt suddenly that he deserved to die. Yes, he wanted to die.

So he walked without thinking, in a kind of blank daze, to the market square. He hailed the first cab he saw and asked to be taken to the Harbour Street.

When he reached the waterfront he got out and walked slowly towards the wharf, unaware of the hardware stores around him, not hearing the solicitations of the whores. At the Royal Mail wharf he passed the sleeping watchman and walked to the quay. Then, step by step, he moved nearer to the end. He forced himself not to think or feel anything. He was enveloped simply with the sole need to end everything; to plunge into the black ocean; to die.

Then at last he reached the end of the quay. He would swim as far out to sea as he could then go down exhausted. One foot went over above the water. But the other remained firmly behind. Soon both feet were back safely on the quay. He had to think again. He felt he had betrayed himself terribly, but he was compelled to think again. Did he want to, really? The answer was obvious even in the asking of the question. To want to die is to die. There are a thousand ways of doing so and if he wanted to he would have done so long ago. The single most salient fact about suicide is its absence of all doubt; its complete denial of life; its absolute certainty. He realised that to ask, do I want to die? is at once to doubt, to be conscious of making a choice between death and something else. And faced with such a situation how else could he choose but that something else since, clearly, death, being the unknown quantity, had to be posed within the terms of that something else.

He stood staring at the water from the edge of the quay. Once more he began to feel the growing sense of self-mockery which sprang from his confrontation with his impossible dishonesty. In his attempt at resolving everything he had once more made what amounted to simply another wild, extravagant, squalid, idiotic gesture. Suicide, death, was the very last thing he desired. Nobody could have loved life as much as he did. It was his very passion for life which led him to make his impossible demands on it. And it was his inevitable dissatisfaction which in turn led him to question the very basis of the life which he desired so much, which he wanted so desperately to give some meaning, to make reasonable and unambiguous.

As he lingered on the quay his sense of sheer stupidity grew more intense and unbearable. Once more he felt that something had to be done. All right, another gesture to cancel the gross foolhardiness of this gesture, perhaps, but anything now would be better than nothing at all.

In sheer desperation he flung himself into the sea. If he was to be a fool he might as well be an absolute fool. And while the going was good he made the most of it by shouting and splashing and screaming, imagining that all Kingston was on the wharf gaping with excitement at him, concerned with his fate. Then he swam back to the shore.

The commotion he had created had woken the watchman, who came charging round the corner of the warehouse, revolver in one hand, flashlight in the other, as soon as Alex pulled himself out of the water.

'A who dat? A who dat? Talk quick or I shoot to kill!' he shouted.

'It's only me,' Alexander answered, rather lamely.

'Me who?'

'Me, Alexander Blackman.'

'And what the rass you doing here? Don't you know is private property?'

'I was only trying to kill myself.'

'Trying to do wharra?'

'You heard what I said: take that damn' light out of my eyes.'

'Trying to kill yourself? You take me for some damn' fool?'

'Not you; myself.'

'Well then, you gain' to pay for your foolhardiness. Ah tekin' you to de water-police station. Move!'

'Good Lord,' Alex said, looking down at himself, 'I'm wet.'

'What de 'ell you expec'? You must be outa you' mind! Come on.'

'I guess they'll have some spare clothes at the station.'

'I'm sure they will. Now you come on.'

At the station Alexander found it simplest to plead that he was drunk and claimed that he had gone to take a bath in order to get sobered up. Unfortunately, he had forgotten to take his clothes off. The constable eyed him suspiciously for some time, but eventually accepted his story and placed him in jail for the night to cool off in some prisoner's garb.

Lying on the bunk in his cell, Alexander finally came around to enquiring of himself why really did he do it. Was it simply for the masochistic thrill of making a fool of himself, or was there, as he suspected, some more important, hidden motive behind it all? After some soul-searching he thought he had found the answer.

It was not himself really whom he wanted to hurt, but those others. If he had killed himself he would have made them all sorry; he would have made the whole world sorry. By committing suicide he would have singled out himself as one of those few who had suffered more, much more than was the ordinary human lot. It was not so much their pity that he needed, but their guilt, their remorse at what they had done to him. Suicide would have been the final, decisive statement absolving him of all responsibility, of all guilt, while at the same time, making them all responsible and guilty for him and his fate. It was, in the final analysis the easy way out, the coward's way out. But, as he had come to realise on the edge of the quay, one had to be courageous in life to be a coward in death. And with Alexander it was quite the other way around. In life, in his confrontation with all the perplexities it had to offer, he was prepared to be the coward, to opt out of everything, to accept responsibility only for himself, and to be responsible only to himself. It was the coward's choice, true. But it was a choice which in its working out, in its logical outcome, implied the courage of refusing death as the solution to anything.

No, it became more and more obvious that this recent flirtation with death was the greatest gesture he had yet made to life. It was prompted by his need to assert once and for all the position he had chosen on life, that of the noble coward. That of someone who refuses to be held responsible; who in his finer moments also refuses to hold anything or anyone responsible for himself, but who, in his baser moments, sought to do exactly the opposite.

And one had to be base sometimes. For him it was an essential part of being human; the necessary recess from the too noble, too demanding, too lonely task of being totally responsible for himself. And as he lay on his bunk, listening to the snoring of his cellmate, he felt that the time had come to be thoroughly base.

Why not, he thought, enjoy the very human pleasures of suicide without suffering the un-human price of it? Why not simply pretend to commit suicide? Yes, by God, he should have thought of that before. He would make them all suffer yet; he would make them all responsible yet. He would spare none of them. His mother perhaps? No! No! She least of all. Furthermore, he felt confident that she could take it. She had not struggled through life all these years for nothing. He would be merciless. He Alexander Blackman, would pass judgement on the whole world. And they shall be punished in their guilt.

# PART THREE

## EXIT, THE SECOND ADAM

>     Ah, why should all Mankind,
> For one man's fault, thus guiltless be condemned?
> If guiltless!…
>
>     All my evasions vain
> And reasonings, though through mazes, lead me still
> But to my own conviction: first and last
> On me, me only, as the source and spring
> Of all corruption, all the blame lights due.

MILTON : *Paradise Lost,* Bk. 10

# 11

The plan was simple. The fact that he was jailed came in quite handy, for it would seem a very plausible last experience of apparent humiliation prompting the fatal act. There had, of course, to be the inevitable suicide note. At first he had grand schemes of giving a long, profound explanation of why he could see no other path but suicide. But he restrained himself when he recalled his recent experience on the edge of the quay. People committing suicide don't really offer explanations. For them it is not so much that life has lost its meaning (an idiotic statement, when Alexander came to think of it) but that meaning itself has lost all meaning; has become totally irrelevant.

No, a genuine suicide note had to have the stamp of something totally fortuitous about it, something that was meaningful only in its complete irrelevance to the issue with which it pretends to be connected. And so it would be with Alexander's note.

He took an old envelope from his wallet, tore off the blank side and wrote, in as hysterical a manner as he could conjure:

'This can't go on. I can't stand it any longer. This is the only way to end it all...'

He paused, wondering whether it would be wiser to end it abruptly, or perhaps to add the usual little touch of sentiment and the appeal for pity. 'I'm sorry, Mother...' he added, and broke off, taking care of the sentiments; then he finished off with the little stroke of self-pity: 'I tried...'

The drunk with whom he had shared the cell for the night turned out to be a willing accomplice when Alexander offered to pay him five pounds to do exactly as he told him. All he was asked to do was to take Alexander's clothes, after he had bought a new set, and keep them for a week. Then he should take both the clothes and the note and hand them to the police, claiming that he had found them abandoned on a deserted part of the waterfront.

Alexander figured that by the end of the week his mother would certainly have reported the fact that he was missing to the police. Having found his clothes and the note, it would be difficult for them not to conclude that he had committed suicide. Doubtless they would check back on the night watchman about the incident on the quay. What really happened? How did he look? What did he say? He was sure that the ordinary Jamaican's love of exaggeration and self-importance would do the rest. He was a lonely man, the old bastard would swear, a sad man, a wretched man. And he did say that...

After drilling his cell-mate for the third time concerning what he should say, Alexander took off to the hills. He knew just the place where he could hide himself, a little village called Jerico, way up in the mountains of Hanover.

He took the train to Montego Bay, then rode on the back of a truck squashed between fifty peasant women with their bundles of crocus bags, baskets and unsold food, returning home from the market. There was some problem getting somewhere to stay in the village, but he finally persuaded a shopkeeper and his woman to put him up.

The village was lost in all the extravagant lushness of the island's interior. It was surrounded by mountains of all heights and patterns. Some scrawled a jagged path along the skyline; others made sharp, stark pyramids, piercing the curdled flocks of white clouds; still others swept overhead forming gigantic lines of elephants. And the colours – how they varied, how they clashed, how they merged into and swallowed up each other. Above the valley the sky was a bald, crisp blue. To the east and west of the mountains facing the village there were greyish-white clouds, both sets of which merged in the centre into deeper, but more moist tones of bluish green. Always above the highest peaks, however, there were the sublimest little fluffs of white clouds. And often this more sedate pattern was pierced by peeping patches of the blue sky.

But what struck Alexander most as he stared out of the

window of the room he had rented were the sharp, contrasting contours of the mountains themselves. An oscillating line humped along the side dividing the top half, which was a hazy blue, from the bottom, which was green with faintly visible vegetation. He had lived in the country for many years and he knew how deceptive was the sight of those hills; he knew how tough, unyielding and infertile the eroded soil was; and, in contrast, how fertile were the large plantations in the valley, with their beautifully laid out banana groves.

That evening he walked down towards the valley, evading the few wooden shops and the thatched, wattle-and-daub habitations of the peasants. Occasionally, when a vehicle came by, he would slip into some cane piece, or behind a yam-hill or silk-cotton tree to avoid being observed. Night caught him on a narrow path, fanned on either side by the vast leaves of seemingly endless rows of banana trees. Sometimes he stopped to listen more closely to the million sounds of the night: the shrill evasive peep of the crickets; the croaking of the frogs; the sudden hysteria of the screech-owls; the graceful swaying of the dew-chilled leaves of the bananas. Standing there, under the clear radiance of the boundless sky, spotted with the frozen glows of countless stars, it was possible for a moment to forget everything, to cease to think or hope or fear. To become again the innocent consciousness of a child; see the world no further up than the knees of adults; live on the undemanding level of green shrubs.

But such romance could last only for a moment. The squeaking of the crickets grew irritatingly monotonous; the mountain air was chilly, making his nose tingle with the need to sneeze. One never knows what desperate, starving peasant, what criminal, lurks behind those broad leaves. Besides, the mosquitoes had begun to bite.

He had asked the shopkeeper to order a copy of the *Daily Gleaner* for him from the van which drove by early in the mornings. Although on the first morning of his disappearance he hardly expected to find any reference to himself, he none the less scanned the newspaper with some excitement.

Finding nothing, he went to the shop, where the owner's wife prepared a cup of coffee for him. Afterwards he bought a bottle of rum, went back to his room, where he had a few drinks, then left for another walk in the cool morning air.

On the road he was passed by a group of peasants. There were five men and three women. The men wore ragged trousers and dirty, torn vests. The women were better clad in wide, baggy skirts and billowy, floral blouses, under which their large breasts, unsupported by bras, heaved and fell with the rhythm of their walk. The men carried hoes over their shoulders and machetes in their other hands. The women had large baskets and crocus-bag bundles on their heads, cushioned by cottas of rolled dried plantain leaves, which, under the weight, flattened the colourful plaid scarves that covered their hair.

Only the soft shifting of the crumpled gravel betrayed their nearness to him. As they passed they murmured a polite good morning.

"Morning,' he answered, then added, 'Going to work your ground, eh?'

'Yes,' they replied, in the same impassive voice.

He walked along behind them, struck by their silence. They walked briskly, but he had the freakish impression that their dark, well-developed limbs moved mechanically, simply covering the same ground they had always covered, doing the same things they had always done, carrying the round heads they had always carried.

They crossed the valley by a path running through the banana field, then started to climb up another, even narrower, path on the hillside facing the village. Alexander followed them, several paces behind. They never looked back at him, although he knew they must have heard him trailing behind them. But they kept their heads straight, each walking behind the other, never altering their pace. It was the feet of the men and the necks of the women which Alexander kept staring at more and more: the broad, thick triangular soles which had long since grown indifferent to the spiky little pieces of white gravel; and the twisted, protruding jugular veins of the short, squashed necks of the women.

On the hillside the vegetation changed dramatically. Here the land was divided up into tiny little quarter-acre lots. Instead of the long, monotonous rows of banana trees which they had just left on the plantation in the valley, here there were plants of every variety – breadfruit, mangoes, yams, plantains, cacaos, peanuts, congo-peas, cashews, the lot. The earth, too, was stony and tough and the trees had a parched stubborn look about them, as if they were all desperately clinging on to life.

Finally, the group he was following reached their ground. It looked like a peanut field, but it may have been red peas. He watched them as they unpacked the bags the women had carried. Then the men went to one side of the little ground and began to dig with their hoes, while the women weeded the yam mounds and the rest of the plot.

Alex refused to believe that they could remain so silent. Were these not his folk? Were they not the happy, simple people of the countryside? Why did they not shout with earthy gusto at each other? Why did they not sing the songs for which they were famous? He asked himself these questions out of sheer self-indulgence, knowing long ago the true character of these peasants.

When, eventually, one of the men did begin to sing, the harsh, weary resignation of his voice did not surprise him; nor did the melancholy dryness of the refrain. It seemed a happy melody, but it was the false happiness of surrender. And the gay rhythm was purely functional, beaten solely to the drumming of the hoe-blade on the tough ground.

He left them, went back to his room, read for the rest of the day, then drank himself to sleep.

The next morning he scanned the newspaper hurriedly, but again found nothing. The same was true of the third morning. He began to grow restless. Could it be that nobody cared? Had his absence gone completely unnoticed? Was he that dispensable? Did he mean that little to them?

On the fourth morning, however, the first notice appeared. 'University man missing', the modest headline on the fifth page read, then went on to explain who he was and how long he had not been seen. There was no mention on the fifth day and Alex, this time, apart from being deflated, began to have doubts about the whole adventure. What was he trying to prove, anyway? What did it matter whether they cared or did not care?

He had begun to pack his bag when the issues became clear to him again. It really was not a matter of whether they cared or not.

The point was to make them responsible and guilty for a change; to make them stand up and say, 'This was a man! A man who bore the burden of his universe upon his own frail shoulders. And we drove him to his death.' He reminded himself that he was on recess; that this was an exercise in baseness, an indulgence of all that was most vile and contemptible in him so that he could appreciate and more accept the virtue of his normal stand. It was indeed a noble act of cowardice. Not since those forty days of Jesus in the wilderness was there a personal exposure such as this.

He saw that his act was totally irresponsible, quite irrational, and possibly even cruel. But he took full responsibility for the moral consequences of his irresponsibility. He owed them nothing; neither mother, nor wife, nor friends. Let them feel the burden of contrition and let them be answerable to him for a change. Perhaps they might even come to say, 'I owe him nothing; I am not responsible.' Then he would have succeeded completely. For he would have changed them. They would begin to see the world the way he did. Then he would have been totally absolved. This apparently mindless venture might yet prove the most rewarding thing he ever did.

On the sixth day of his disappearance the news once more appeared in the newspapers. This time it was promoted to the third page and had a photograph of him which he had given to his mother after graduating from university.

The same picture with the same description appeared the next day. It was the same day that his former cell-mate had been told to deliver the clothes and note and throughout he fidgeted restlessly. That night he hardly slept with excitement. At one point, near midnight, he had a spell of cold feet and was on the point of sending his mother a telegram.

But he remained strong. This was the greatest moral battle of his life. Here, at last, he was faced with genuine issues. At last he had come face to face with morality. No longer was it a lifeless, phoney abstraction bounded within the pretentious volumes of philosophers. Now it had acquired flesh and blood, had become subjectively meaningful; something he felt running through his veins and which gripped him with excitement.

He was faced with concrete issues and had to choose between equally concrete alternatives. Should he or should he not reveal himself at this point? If he revealed himself he had some sort of compensation in the fact that he would possibly have saved their suffering and their guilt; but at the same time he would have been totally dishonest, for he genuinely felt no responsibility for others, least of all for their own sufferings and responsibilities. On the other hand, should he not reveal himself, he would have remained perfectly honest (partly in his self-conscious indulgence of his baseness) and, who knows, even have changed them for the better.

And firm he remained. By the eighth morning his mind was fully made up. His temptations, so to speak (for he had developed quite a liking for the analogy), were virtually over. It was with great satisfaction that he read on the front page of the newspaper, in most distinguished headlines, 'Former lecturer suspected suicide'. The story gave the relevant details about the clothes and the note, then went on to give a not unflattering account of his 'short and tragic life'.

*Mr. Alexander Blackman, the only son of Miss Rebecca Jones, is believed to have committed suicide by drowning himself on Wednesday of last week. Mr. Blackman, who was well known until recently, in literary and political circles, graduated from the William Wilberforce Memorial High School and went to the University of the West Indies after being awarded a Centenary scholarship. He took a first in social sciences and then proceeded in 1953 to Oxford University on a Rhodes scholarship where he did a doctoral dissertation on 'The Contribution of the Negro to Western Civilisation.' After leaving Oxford Mr. Blackman, in 1956, returned to the University of the West Indies where he joined the academic staff and, a few months later, married the former Miss Pauline Richards. In 1957 Mr. Blackman returned to England where he taught for two years, and finally, in June last year rejoined the staff of the University of the West Indies. It is reported that ever since he returned he has been increasingly depressed about what one colleague described as 'the human condition.' Mr. Blackman is also said to have been generally disillusioned about politics, literature, and even his own academic discipline. He suddenly resigned his post at the*

*University in May of this year and has gradually dropped out of all public life since then. He was separated from his wife when the fatal incident took place. Many friends and well-wishers have sent their warmest sympathies to Miss Jones concerning the short and tragic life of her very talented son. His body has not yet been recovered.*

And so the deed was done. His death was now a reality to everyone except himself. Now they would all be forced to sit up and think. Even the most indifferent of them could not help but ask why he did it? And once they had asked why, they would, even in the smallest way, have assumed some responsibility. To even the most stupid and insensitive the issues must have been painfully clear. He had killed himself; he had not found life worth living; for him life had become meaningless. They on the other hand were still very much alive; they had chosen to live and so to them life was worth while and meaningful. Therefore they had a stake in life and by living it they were responsible for what it was. Ergo, they were partly responsible for him not finding it possible to accept it. Sure they would quickly disown all responsibility by claiming it was his own choice to kill himself. But in the very act of defending themselves they would condemn themselves. The very fact that they were still very much alive would give their rationalisation the lie. Then they would be angry at him for killing himself. And being angry about something which they felt they ought to feel sympathy for would then lead them on to guilt. Ah, how he had trapped them! How wonderful it was to feel and know that at last the whole world had been made to care, to feel responsible, to be guilty about oneself.

All that day Alexander walked about the mountains a god among the trees. He was sure he felt the way Jehovah feels in his knowledge that he was the source of all morality, and that he alone could pass judgement. For was not that what he had done? Had he not passed judgement on them all? Had he not entered their innermost souls and beaten them with the rod of guilt?

'How many are the days of thy servant? When wilt thou execute judgement on them that persecute me?'

When, like the author of the psalm, he was mortal, he had

130

asked that same question. Now the belief in his death had made him a kind of god, and in that very belief he had passed judgement on them.

That night he lay on his back, staring blissfully at the ceiling. In the distance he could hear the voices of the peasants in their church. He heard the shouting of the preacher; and then the harsh, ecstatic spasms of their possession by the spirit. And he listened to the rhythm of the drums and the shaking of the tambourines, as they sung their songs of worship:

*Are your garments spotless?*
*Are they white as snow?*
*Are they washed in the blood of the Lamb?*
*Oh, are your garments spotless?*
*Are they white as snow?*
*Are you washed in the blood of the Lord...*

The next morning he woke up a little less elated. There was no mention of him in the newspaper, but it did not matter, for he thought he had already achieved his end. The problem now of his 'resurrection' began to worry him a little. In the excitement of initiating and executing his plan of judgement he had neglected what he considered then to be the relatively minor problem of telling the world he had played a moral hoax on it. In the end he thought there was nothing else he could do but simply to reappear and so he decided he would return home the next day.

He was having the usual cup of coffee the following morning in the bar behind the shop when the grocer's wife asked him if he was interested in seeing the morning paper that had been left for him. He thanked her and explained that he had forgotten about it. Lazily he scanned the pages, hardly expecting to find any mention of himself, when he was shocked by the following headline on the third page:

'Mother collapses after news of son's suicide.' The story ran briefly:

*Miss Rebecca Jones, mother of the late Alexander Blackman, who is believed to have committed suicide last Wednesday, collapsed at her*

*residence yesterday. She is believed to have suffered a coronary throm-*
*bosis brought on by the shock and strain of the news of her son's death.*
*She was rushed by relatives to the Kingston Public Hospital and her*
*condition is considered critical.*

He read the story over and over again, not daring to believe it. Then he sprang from his seat shouting, 'No! No! It is not possible.' He ran to his room to collect his things, then went back to the shopkeeper, asking her where he could send a telegram. The nearest post office was in the next village. He paid off his bill to the grocer's wife, then began walking towards the other village, hoping to get a lift on the way. Only a lorry came along the road and it did not stop.

An hour later, having walked all the way, he had given the message to the girl behind the counter of the post office. It ran simply : 'I am alive. It was all a big mistake. Will be home tonight', but he had no guarantee as to when the telegram would arrive, since the postmistress, he was maliciously informed, the only person who knew how to send a telegram, had just left with the Anglican parson, not saying where she was destined.

It was another three hours before he had managed to get a ride on a truck and cleared the mountains and when he arrived in Montego Bay he discovered that he would have to wait for the six o'clock train. He took his chances on getting a lift into Kingston and was fortunate, a half an hour later, to receive one in a large American car driven by an elderly civil servant.

As he drove along he realised that everything had collapsed. He had succeeded in being base and contemptible; but it was not quite the way he had intended it. Nothing ever seemed to work out the way he wanted it. She was not meant to die. To suffer a little, to feel guilty, perhaps. But not to die. For if she did the whole world would have held him responsible. He, not they, would now be guilty. They now would pass judgement on him.

But that was exactly what he wanted. This is what frightened him most. He realised, with increasing revulsion, that he did want to be responsible, to be guilty. But the horrors of what this implied he could not confront. For did it not mean that he wanted her to die? No. This was not possible. Something had gone wrong in his reasoning. He wanted her to live! He wanted her to live! he kept hammering into his conscience.

But it was no longer possible to be dishonest. Not, in any case, with something such as death. He knew what he wanted. To be absolutely responsible, to be totally guilty. Well, that was one way of putting it. But his consciousness of the means (the murder of his mother) by which he was attaining his objective, itself added yet a further dimension to his guilt. Thus he was guilty in the attainment of his guilt.

At the same time, he still remained human. And it was human to feel guilt in somebody else's, especially a mother's, death; the guilt which comes from the feeling that you are not as sympathetic as you feel you ought to be. And this kind of guilt he patently did not experience. So he was also guilty in the absence of the attainment of his guilt.

As the car sped along he became more and more conscious of his complete dishonesty. What was the urgency? Why had he explained to the driver that his mother was dying and asked him to drive faster? Why did he want to reach her side? Slowly his being became limp with the ravages of the contradictions within him. Then, mercifully, everything gradually became numb and deadened; conscience, thought and feeling were temporarily paralysed. For the rest of the journey he discussed the latest developments in the Test match between England and the West Indies with the driver.

There was a small group of relatives and close friends sitting in the living room when he arrived. As soon as he dashed inside he could feel that everything had changed. The all-pervasive sense of absence was almost tangible. It was in the stillness of everything. The flowers in the vase seemed artificial, though he knew his mother always kept fresh flowers. The limp curtains, the chairs, and the people sitting in them all seemed severed, unrelated to anything. But it was the stillness of their countenances which seemed most articulate. The vacant gape of bewilderment which comes with the realisation that one is confronted with something against which one remains powerless and impotent.

Aunt Clarissa, his mother's sister, was still holding the telegram when he came in. She looked up at him and for a moment an air of confusion overcame her. Then she looked back down at the telegram. 'We thought someone was playing a cruel hoax…' she began, then suddenly seemed to have realised what she had just seen. 'Alexander!' she shouted, then screamed.

The other two women in the room had just kept staring at him in a dazed kind of disbelief. Then from the bedroom another woman and his uncle, a tall, powerfully built man, the darkest of his mother's relatives, hurried out. They stood their ground at the door and joined the other three in gaping at him. It was his uncle who finally broke the silence. In a muffled voice, which sounded too shocked to be spoken beyond a whisper, he asked:

'What in the name of God is this? Didn't they say you were dead?'

His uncle's voice rang with suspicion and anger. He had never liked Alexander, claiming that too much studying had made him cold and ungrateful, if not slightly mad. He was himself a very illiterate man with a nasty temper and a heavy chip on his shoulder.

'You know what you done?' he continued in the same tone of astonishment. 'You know what you gone an' done? You kill your mother. Jesus Christ Almighty! You kill your mother, boy!'

He stared around at the women in disbelief. To each of them he said, as if he needed their confirmation that the words he was uttering were indeed true: 'The boy kill 'im mother. You hear what me say, the boy kill 'im mother. Me say, the boy kill 'im mother.'

Each time he said that crippling phrase his voice grew louder and louder, and trembled more and more with rage. He began to walk menacingly towards Alexander, his bloodshot eyes becoming once more moist with tears.

'She… she isn't dead,' Alexander said helplessly, more to himself than anyone else.

'She's dead,' his uncle suddenly screamed, 'an' you kill her.' As he said the last word he pounced on Alexander, held him round his chest, and flung him to the ground. Then he lifted him up and began to pummel him mercilessly, screaming on the top of his voice, 'You kill her! You kill your own mother! I'm going to murder you!'

Alexander gave in to the battering. Each time the heavy hand of his uncle crashed into his teeth and his eyes he winced with pain. Yet he did not resist. It was not just that he felt he deserved it, but that he wanted to be beaten, to be stricken, to be killed. As he tasted the salt of his own blood, as his head reeled and swelled with the pressure of his uncle's large palms squeezing round his neck, he realised that this, perhaps, would have been the best way to end it all. He was about to pass out in the sweet agony of pain when he heard the women screaming, and could barely discern his uncle being pulled from off him by them. Suddenly they had all grown large, and out of all proportion. The women were like great distorted Amazons in a dream, pulling some mighty dragon from him. They all melted into one, large, vague amorphous greyish-black form, curling in and out like the fumes of anguish. Then they faded away.

He could not have passed out for very long, for when he regained consciousness under the stimulant of Aunt Clarissa's smelling salts, his uncle was still panting like a tired bulldog on the chair opposite to where he lay.

'Where is she?' he asked her as soon as he had sufficient energy.

'In there,' she said, pointing. He got up painfully and stumbled to his mother's bedroom. He closed the door behind him and leaned against it. Everything else in the room seemed to have diminished in size. Her bed loomed large and awesome over everything. The more he stared, the more everything in the background retreated, till he saw only a humped form shrouded in white linen.

He walked up to the bedside and, without pausing to think how he would react, he pulled away the cloth from her face. Her expression was a quaint mixture of relaxation and anguish. Her flesh, without the life in it, could not help but appear flaccid and freakishly composed. For a brief moment he even failed to recognise her; so used had he become to her tenseness, her permanent sense of loss. Yet at the same time there was the slightest intimation of a little touch of grasping, as if, just before dying, she had wished to say or do something. To cry a little more, perhaps.

He re-covered her face and left the room, his being too numb to record the pain his body must still have felt. He passed the people in the living room, glimpsing their mute forms like shades in the afternoon. Then he wandered aimlessly upon the dry plot where she had spent so many vain hours trying to preserve her lawn from the onslaught of the sun. Only when he bumped into the fence did he fully realise that he was outside.

He moved towards the gate, went on to the street, and walked towards the sea. At the end of the road he stopped and stared blankly at the water. He did not hear the startled gasp of the woman beside him or even when she called his name the first time.

'Alexander!' she said again.

He looked round and saw Pauline standing beside him.

'Oh, it's you…'

'Where have you been! What happened?'

'It was all a pretence… I pretended to commit suicide. Don't ask me why I did it. I don't feel like explaining.'

'But you…'

'Yes, I know; I killed her. Say what you like.'

'My God! But it is not possible.'

He did not answer her. After a long silence he suddenly turned to her and asked out of idle curiosity: 'Did you think I had killed myself too?'

'I didn't believe it at first. But afterwards the evidence…'

'And how did you respond? Don't lie to me. You don't have to lie to criminals.'

'Don't you feel any remorse? How can you enquire about yourself…'

'Answer me! Answer me! I can only think about myself if I am not to go crazy thinking about everything else.'

She continued to stare at him in astonishment.

'Well then, what happened? How did you respond to the news of my suicide?'

She continued to stare at him a while longer. Then her face softened a bit as she began to feel some pity for him.

'Well, if you must know… if I must be truthful… what I felt most was relief. I'm sorry…'

'There is nothing to be sorry about. Go on.'

'Well… how can I put it. I felt free. You suddenly weren't there any more. I was forced to face that. And in facing it I realised at last that I didn't need you any more. That in fact I hadn't needed you for a long time past…'

'And after that?'

'Must I give you all the gory details?'

'Every bit of it. Furthermore, I know you're enjoying it. You have every right to, of course.'

'Well, later the same afternoon that I heard the news, Edward came back around – it was he who had broken the news to me. He came ostensibly to console me. But he soon discovered that I had little need for consolation. I was crying, but he didn't take long to sense that I wasn't crying with grief. So he… he began to kiss me. Then everything in me suddenly went ablaze. I dragged him down on the floor right there in the living room. It was almost cathartic, that act. I've never experienced anything so physical and so… Well, whatever the word is. All at the same time. Release! That's it. I had a sense of complete release. We've been sleeping with each other since. Of course, I know this sudden sense of freedom – this pleasure in simply living – won't go on for very long. Already when I get up in the mornings I have begun to have the doubts about myself, about everything, that I used to have. But at least now I have the courage to face them myself. Funny how, in gaining complete independence from you, I have at last found it possible to be a little like you.'

'Don't be so sure.'

'What do you mean?'

'I mean about me; about the things I used to say; about the things I used to pretend to believe. I caused her death. I am responsible for her death. What I believe in has finally been put to the test. And I can't accept it. I can't bear to believe that I caused it. I am prepared to accept the responsibility for everything except what I know I must accept. Dear God, is it possible to be more dishonest?…'

'I'm going home now,' she said. 'I don't think your family quite approves of me at this moment. Besides, there is nothing to say to them.'

'Can I stay with you a while?'

'Well… Edward was coming around tonight…'

'Please, I must go somewhere. It will be no more than a couple of days. I simply want to be able to go to the funeral.'

'And then?'

'I'll take the first plane I can get?'

'Well, I guess we're not yet divorced, which reminds me…'

They buried her the next afternoon in the May Pen Cemetery. It was a small funeral. A few friends of what, with some imagination, could have been called the family came along: Miss Pearl, Mr. Jackson, Mass Rufus and T. T. Brown. There was also this short, barrel-shaped brown man, with large, plaintive, greyish-black eyes, who suddenly popped up from nowhere, claiming to be Alexander's father, and who kept apologising, almost compulsively, to everyone, although it was not clear exactly what for.

And, of course, there was his Uncle Colin, who never took his glowering, accusing eyes off Alexander's. There was Aunt Jane, who insisted that they sung the hymn, 'I am only a visitor here, Lord, I am only a visitor here.' And there was Aunt Clarissa, who cried.

## 12

Edward and Pauline are making love in the next room. I can hear the rubbing and the slapping of their flesh. I can hear his deep sadistic grunts. And I can hear her masochistic moans of pleasure. I have never known her to cry out so much in lovemaking and cannot help feeling that it is partly meant for me to hear. Well, if it increases her pleasure, all the better for her. Their groans and deep gasps of passion are simply sounds in the night to me. If I listen to them it is only in a vain attempt to prevent myself from hearing my own thoughts.

At last I am exposed. Her death has filled me with shame. And my shame has exposed me to what I really am. For suddenly it has betrayed my guiltlessness. Me, of all persons. My guilt with which I was so obsessed, which had become the pivot of my being, I now see as a sham. I even begin to doubt whether it was ever there. This, perhaps, was the real absence, the hidden emptiness which lay behind everything. And what a fool I was not to have known it. To think, not only did I fail to recognise its absence, but had fooled myself into thinking that it formed the essence of my being. I who sought never to be excused had created this great fiction of my life to excuse everything.

How simple and crude it all now appears. How totally contemptible. I could be cruel, I could disown the consequences not only of my actions but of everything I was, my involvement in life itself. It was sufficient simply to convince myself that I was guilty, and in being thus convinced I was assured of my punishment and, no less, that I was absolved. Was there anyone who so ignominiously had their cake and ate it?

In the end it becomes clear that I never confronted anything.

Loneliness, anxiety, meaninglessness, responsibility, were merely intimated, simply vague abstractions peeped at through the key-hole of this fraudulent guilt behind which I cowered.

Yet the big question remains. If what I felt was not guilt, then what was it? For surely I did experience something. Must I believe that the entries of this diary are all lies, all part of the elaborate fable which formed the basis of my evasion? Surely, if I am such an absolute coward, if I could stoop so low as to murder my mother without any real contrition, why did I find it necessary to create this great myth of my guilt? Could the answer be that to be human one has to meet the minimal requirement of at least wanting to be guilty? And I suppose that in the same way the slum-dweller in the shanty town of this city is degraded into a complete obsession with the material things of life by his very lack of them, so was I degraded into this obsession with the minimalities of guilt by my very lack of it.

And it is my dishonesty, which I have tried so much to hide, that has at last betrayed me. It has revealed me not only to the world, which is the least of my embarrassment, for I am too indifferent now to care for the accusing stare of an illiterate uncle, or the contempt of a one-time wife and her lover making love in the next room; what is so much worse is that it has revealed me to myself. And I can only squirm with self-embarrassment at what I see – the squalid, incongruous fool I am.

There is little point in probing much further; certainly it would be taking self-mockery too far to make another entry in this diary. No longer could I bring myself to question anything again; for now it is I who have become so utterly questionable. No longer can I play about with meaning, for it is clear that I can never take such probing seriously. It is not that like the person about to commit suicide meaning has lost all relevance for me. This may be so, but to the person who commits suicide this irrelevance is a deathly serious business. I, on the other hand, approach the irrelevance of meaning from the very opposite pole; from the shadows of the woodpile, so to speak, with the comic clamour of excited fowls and the indignant rage of fascists in the background. It is not just meaning or its irrelevance which isn't taken seriously, but the approach itself, the approach of the thief who is never quite taken seriously, whether caught or not.

It is no longer, then, that I find life worthless, but that life has found me worthless. I have been caught naked; unexpectedly. I see myself in the mirror of my shame and I flush and turn myself away, for I am impotent, cowardly, abandoned and incongruous.

Is there no place where I can hide? Is there no dark jungle among whose tangled trees I can get myself lost for ever? Is there no vast, indifferent horde somewhere amongst which I can sink and drown in anonymity?

## PART FOUR

## THE EPILOGUE

It was not only that I could not become spiteful, I did not know how to become anything: neither spiteful nor kind, neither a rascal nor an honest man, neither a hero nor an insect. Now, I am living out my life in my corner, taunting myself with the spiteful and useless consolation that an intelligent man cannot become anything seriously, and it is only the fool who becomes anything.

DOSTOEVSKY : *Notes from Underground*

…in London city, if on a cold December evening you see emerging from the foggy shadows of some narrow, grey-bricked alley, a faceless figure, gaunt, mute and mechanical in movement; or, if, meandering in the Underground with the vacant crowd of a late afternoon, a stiff, blank face appears just that little bit too much a part of the hurrying horde, so that it betrays itself as being somehow apart… Take notice! Observe him carefully. For he is a rare chameleon. A being deprived of essence. The willing slave of every chance event.

Only once was he spotted by a curious sharp-eyed native of the city, who stopped him in the street and said:

'Wait, I wish to question you. Tell us who you are. You have the appearance of the savage, yet you would pretend to be exactly like us; so much so indeed that often your actions and your manner blind us to your appearance making us think that you are one of us. What manner of man are you? Where do you come from? What of your past? Who are your ancestors? Are you savage or are you civilised? Identify yourself, sir! Tell us who you are and where it is you always seem to be in such a great hurry to be going. For we are a practical, straightforward race, and cannot tolerate such ambiguities in our midst.'

Then, looking with his remote eyes at the enquiring native, and in a voice devoid of all emotion, this strange man replied:

'I come from nowhere worth mentioning. I have no past, except the haunting recollection of each passing moment which comes to me always as something having lost. My ancestors, if they existed, left no record of themselves; my mother who also fathered me, I sacrificed to a futile cause many shameful years ago. If I appear to be like you, please understand that it is out of no vain wish to be identified with you, but out of the simple desire not to draw attention to myself. I cannot say whether I am civilised or savage, standing as I do outside of race, outside of culture, outside of history, outside of any value that could make your question meaningful. I am busy going nowhere, but I must keep up the appearance of going in order to forget that I am not. So if you'll excuse me, I will be on my way.'

# ABOUT THE AUTHOR

Orlando Patterson was born in Westmoreland, Jamaica, in 1940. He grew up in Clarendon in the little town of Maypen. After completing primary school there, he moved to Kingston to attend Kingston College. He went on to earn a BSc in Economics from the University of the West Indies at Mona in 1962, and a PhD at the London School of Economics in 1965. After teaching sociology at the London School of Economics for two years he returned to the University of the West Indies as a lecturer in Sociology in 1967. In 1970 he left Jamaica to take a position as Visiting Associate Professor at Harvard where he is now John Cowles Professor of Sociology. Patterson was also, for eight years, Special Advisor for Social Policy and Development to Prime Minister Michael Manley of Jamaica. He wrote a guest column for several weeks with the *New York Times*.

Orlando Patterson is the author of three novels, and numerous well-respected academic works on questions of slavery and race. His short stories, essays and reviews have appeared in a variety of journals and anthologies. He received the First Prize for Fiction for *The Children of Sisyphus* at the Dakar Festival of Negro Arts in 1966. He also won the National Book Award for Non-Fiction in 1991 for his *Freedom and the Making of Western Culture*. He holds honorary degrees from several universities, including the University of Chicago, U.C.L.A and La Trobe University in Australia. He was awarded the Order of Distinction by the Government of Jamaica in 1999.

# ALSO BY ORLANDO PATTERSON

*Children of Sisyphus*
ISBN 9781845230944; pp. 216; May 2012; £9.99.
Introduction: Kwame Dawes

The Dungle is a rubbish heap in West Kingston, where the very poorest squat. It is the home of Dinah, a prostitute who has the ambition to escape; Mary, who invests her dreams and her body in her daughter's education; and Brother Soloman, a black, defrocked priest who has come to find the god within amongst the Rastafarians. Patterson's portrayal of the Rastafarians is exact and empathetic, but deeply questioning.

No less shocking now than when it was published nearly fifty years ago, not least because the violence Patterson portrays has undoubtedly grown worse, this novel is much more than an extraordinarily vivid piece of social realism, because Patterson, the reader of Camus, Sartre and Frantz Fanon, invests his characters with complex personalities and motivations, not least the urge to question the nature of their existence. Their voices are presented with all the urgency, poetry and idiomatic directness of urban Jamaican speech that predicts the reggae revolution of the 1970s.

In keeping with Camus's heroic image of the mythical Sisyphus, the novel, for all its dread bleakness, holds onto the idea of faith in betterment as the sustaining force in the Jamaican psyche.

# CARIBBEAN MODERN CLASSICS

Now in print:

Wayne Brown, *On The Coast*
ISBN 9781845231507, pp. 115, £8.99
Introduction: Mervyn Morris

George Campbell, *First Poems*
ISBN: 9781845231491, pp.177, £.9.99
Introduction: Kwame Dawes

Jan Carew, *Black Midas*
ISBN 9781845230951, pp.272 £8.99
Introduction: Kwame Dawes

Jan Carew, *The Wild Coast*
ISBN 9781845231101, pp. 240; £8.99
Introduction: Jeremy Poynting

Austin Clarke, *Amongst Thistles and Thorns*
ISBN 9781845231477, pp.208; £8.99
Introduction: Aaron Kamugisha

Austin Clarke, *Survivors of the Crossing*
ISBN 9781845231668, pp. 208; £9.99
Introduction: Aaron Kamugisha

Neville Dawes, *The Last Enchantment*
ISBN 9781845231170, pp. 332; £9.99
Introduction: Kwame Dawes

Wilson Harris, *Heartland*
ISBN 9781845230968, pp. 104; £7.99
Introduction: Michael Mitchell

Wilson Harris, *The Eye of the Scarecrow*
ISBN 9781845231644, pp. 118, £7.99
Introduction: Michael Mitchell

George Lamming, *Of Age and Innocence*
ISBN 9781845231453, pp. 436, £14.99
Introduction: Jeremy Poynting

Earl Lovelace, *While Gods Are Falling*
ISBN 9781845231484, pp. 258; £10.99
Introduction: J. Dillon Brown

Una Marson, *Selected Poems*
ISBN 9781845231682, pp. 184; £9.99
Introduction: Alison Donnell

Edgar Mittelholzer, *Corentyne Thunder*
ISBN 9781845231118, pp. 242; £8.99
Introduction: Juanita Cox

Edgar Mittelholzer, *A Morning at the Office*
ISBN 9781845230661, pp.210; £9.99
Introduction: Raymond Ramcharitar

Edgar Mittelholzer, *Shadows Move Among Them*
ISBN 9781845230913, pp. 358; £12.99
Introduction: Rupert Roopnaraine

Edgar Mittelholzer, *The Life and Death of Sylvia*
ISBN 9781845231200, pp. 366; £12.99
Introduction: Juanita Cox

Elma Napier, *A Flying Fish Whispered*
ISBN: 9781845231026; pp. 248; July 2010; £9.99
Introduction: Evelyn O'Callaghan

Orlando Patterson, *Children of Sisyphus*
ISBN 9781845230944; pp. 216; May 2012; £9.99
Introduction: Kwame Dawes

Andrew Salkey, *Escape to an Autumn Pavement*
ISBN 9781845230982, pp. 220; £8.99
Introduction: Thomas Glave

Andrew Salkey, *Hurricane*
ISBN 9781845231804, pp. 101, £6.99

Andrew Salkey, *Earthquake*
ISBN 9781845231828, pp. 103, £6.99

Andrew Salkey, *Drought*
ISBN 9781845231835, pp. 121, £6.99

Andrew Salkey, *Riot*
ISBN 9781845231811, pp. 174, £7.99

Garth St Omer, *A Room on the Hill*
ISBN 9781845230937, pp. 168, £8.99
Introduction: Jeremy Poynting

Denis Williams, *Other Leopards*
ISBN 9781845230678, pp. 216; £8.99
Introduction: Victor Ramraj

Denis Williams, *The Third Temptation*
ISBN 9781845231163, pp. 108; £8.99
Introduction: Victor Ramraj

Titles thereafter include...

O.R. Dathorne, *The Scholar Man*
O.R. Dathorne, *Dumplings in the Soup*
Neville Dawes, *Interim*
Wilson Harris, *The Sleepers of Roraima*
Wilson Harris, *Tumatumari*
Wilson Harris, *Ascent to Omai*
Wilson Harris, *The Age of the Rainmakers*
Marion Patrick Jones, *Panbeat*
Marion Patrick Jones, *Jouvert Morning*
George Lamming, *Water With Berries*
Roger Mais, *Black Lightning*
Edgar Mittelholzer, *Children of Kaywana*
Edgar Mittelholzer, *The Harrowing of Hubertus*
Edgar Mittelholzer, *Kaywana Blood*
Edgar Mittelholzer, *My Bones and My Flute*
Edgar Mittelholzer, *A Swarthy Boy*
V.S. Reid, *The Leopard* (North America only)
Garth St. Omer, *Shades of Grey*
Andrew Salkey, *The Late Emancipation of Jerry Stover*
and more...